# Hope in My Heart

# Hope in My Heart

A Collection of *Heartwarming* Stories

ALEXIS A. GORING

CROSSBOOKS
PUBLISHING

CrossBooks™
A Division of LifeWay
1663 Liberty Drive
Bloomington, IN 47403
www.crossbooks.com
Phone: 1-866-879-0502

First published by CrossBooks 09/04/2013

ISBN: 978-1-4627-3114-5 (sc)
ISBN: 978-1-4627-3112-1 (hc)
ISBN: 978-1-4627-3113-8 (e)

Library of Congress Control Number: 2013915709

Printed in the United States of America.

This book is printed on acid-free paper.

Any people depicted in stock imagery provided by Thinkstock are models,
and such images are being used for illustrative purposes only.

Certain stock imagery © Thinkstock.

Cover design: McClearen Design Studios
http://www.mcclearendesign.com/

*This book is dedicated to:*

*Everyone who has hope in their heart,*
*Keep pushing for your dream to come true.*

# ACKNOWLEDGEMENTS

*My gratitude goes to God, who gave me the gift of writing, and to my parents, who believe in my dreams and are willing to help me make them come true.*

*I want to thank all of my family members who encourage me to reach for the stars.*

*My dear grandma deserves recognition for patiently listening to my stories and providing feedback about my characters and the plot.*

*I am deeply appreciative of my church family, especially those who prayed this project through the production process.*

*Sally Bradley, my editor, thank you for helping me perfect this novella.*

*Thank you to Brenda and your team at McClearen Design Studios for creating such a beautiful cover for my book.*

*Finally, here's to everyone who believes in me. You know who you are, and I appreciate you from the depths of my heart.*

# Book One:

## *Love Unexpected*

*Love Unexpected*

# Chapter 1

Sebastian Carter stretched out his muscles then flexed in the gym mirror. "What's cooking, good looking?" he asked his reflection.

"Aren't you tired of talking to yourself?" Someone snapped a towel against Sebastian's chiseled arms. "Get a girlfriend!"

Sebastian flashed a grin to his gym buddy, Hannah Sutton. "You busy Saturday night?"

Hannah rolled her eyes. "Yeah, I'm busy all right." She flashed her ring finger in the mirror, and the glare of a diamond blinded him for a second.

"What?" He shielded his eyes. "When did this happen?"

"Yesterday," Hannah replied with a sigh.

"Congratulations. Who's the lucky man?"

A deep blush colored Hannah's face.

"Oh," Sebastian teased, "so he makes you blush! Must be somebody special."

A male voice sounded behind Sebastian. "Hey, what are you doing talking to *my* fiancée, Sebastian?"

Sebastian turned to see Hannah's personal trainer, Jacob Richards, standing beside him. Sebastian laughed. "Naw, naw! You two are a couple now?"

Jacob walked past him and encircled Hannah in his arms. The

deep blush on Hannah's face was replaced with a beautiful glow as she and Jacob shared a look and then a kiss.

"Aww, no, man," Sebastian cried. "Save the PDA for another place and time."

But Hannah and Jacob were oblivious to his pleas. He shielded his eyes from the newly engaged couple and made his way toward the locker room. First his sister got married. Sebastian glanced over his shoulder at Hannah and Jacob, walking arm-in-arm toward the treadmills. And now his best gym buddy. What was going on?

"There must be something in the water," he mused then paused. "In that case, I'm showering at home."

*Love Unexpected*

# Chapter 2

"Essie!"

Esmeralda Rodriguez looked up from her desk to see her assistant, Chandra McIntire, run into her corner office and pause to gather her breath. "Yes, Chandra?" she asked.

Chandra was one of Esmeralda's favorite workers. Five years ago, Chandra had secured an internship with Boulevard Fashions and now worked exclusively with Esmeralda.

Chandra was five feet four, very petite, and personable. Everyone at the fashion agency liked her, but sometimes her dramatic panic attacks, generated by the daily deadlines, frazzled her colleagues.

"What is it, Chandra?"

Chandra held up her hand as if to say, "Wait a minute," and sat down in the chair in front of Esmeralda's desk. "You won't believe it."

Esmeralda grew calm, preparing herself for any news of a crisis or another wave of Chandra's dramatic flairs.

"*Prima and Primo* wants to stop by the office and see you!"

Esmeralda felt her eyes grow wide. "Shut up."

Chandra shook her head. "I'm *serious.*" Prima and Primo was a premier design firm based in Southern California and were quickly gaining nationwide publicity with their cutting edge, fancy, but affordable fashions.

5

Esmeralda nearly dropped the folder she held. Quickly, she placed it on her desk and took out her Blackberry. "When?" *I've got to make room for this,* she thought as she checked her phone agenda.

"Today."

Esmeralda dropped everything. "Stop lying!"

Chandra shook her thick, dark brown curls to say she wasn't lying and smiled.

"What time? Where? Why? Oh my—I've got to fix my hair!" Esmeralda cried as she adjusted her messy-style hair bun while looking in the mirror attached to her wall.

"I told them that you would be free this afternoon."

"Time, Chandra. What *time?*"

"Five o'clock."

"All right, I think I can be ready by then." Esmeralda picked up her Blackberry again to pencil in the meeting. "Why so late?" she asked, looking up at Chandra.

"They want to take us out to dinner."

"Us?" Esmeralda questioned. "As in who?"

"Me and you," Chandra replied then gave her boss a more serious look. "Honestly now, do you think I would let an opportunity like this pass me by?"

Esmeralda laughed. "Okay then. We'll be ready. Did they share the meeting's agenda with you?"

Chandra shrugged. "They said they would like to discuss the nature of this meeting over a meal."

"Did they let you pick the restaurant?"

"Yes."

"And you chose . . . "

"Sunset Boulevard Grill."

"All right. Sounds good."

As Chandra exited, Esmeralda finished entering the business dinner date into her Blackberry. Prima and Primo . . . she couldn't wait to find out what they wanted with her company.

~ \* ~

*Monday evening, 6:00 p.m.*

Esmeralda leaned forward from her posh chair to kindly address Geraldina Ruiz and Jonathan Ruiz of Prima and Primo. "Thank you so much for inviting my assistant and me to this business dinner."

"Oh, believe me when I say that it is our honor to be dining with such a reputable force in the marketing industry," Geraldina returned.

Esmeralda was flattered. "Thank you, Dina. We are honored by your presence."

"Dinner was *amazing*," Chandra said, speaking of their four-course meal.

Geraldina directed her attention to Chandra. "Tell me, how long have you been working for this famous marketing maven?"

Chandra, whose eyes were fixed on the dessert menu, looked up and smiled. "Five years."

"Good for you. I don't believe I've kept an assistant for more than two years. It's like they get the experience then move on to greater things."

"Oh, but Geraldina," Esmeralda interrupted. "You are such a visionary. I have no doubt your assistants are inspired and honored to work for you even if it's only for a little while."

Geraldina smiled. "Speaking of vision, let's talk about my vision for a fashion show to be marketed by your firm."

At the mention of a possible collaboration with Dina and Jon, Esmeralda's eyes lit up, for it was her dream. "I'm all ears."

Dina and her business partner Jon shared a look. "You say it best," Jon said, allowing Dina to explain her vision.

"I want to do a show featuring my latest designs for the spring season which is part of fashion week. I want your company to be responsible for the marketing and perhaps even help me pick the models for the runway. What do you say?"

Esmeralda and Chandra shared look of pure excitement then faced their new business partners and said in unison, "We'd love to work with you!"

*Love Unexpected*

# Chapter 3

"**B**rother!" Daisy Carter-Reyes greeted her older brother at the front door of her new townhouse.

"Hey, sis!" Sebastian gave Daisy a bear hug. "Where's Enrique?"

"He went with his boys to a baseball game."

"Without me?"

Daisy laughed. "You can't always hang out with the guys, SB. Get a girlfriend, bro. You're thirty."

"Why is everyone telling me to get a girlfriend and reminding me of my age?"

Daisy shrugged. "Maybe because we care about you and don't want to see you lonely."

"Please," Sebastian scoffed. "The ladies *love* me."

"Then why," Daisy countered, "don't you go steady with one special lady?"

"*Because*," Sebastian said, running a hand over his smooth, bald head as he looked in the mirror placed on the wall in Daisy's foyer. "I love me."

"Yeah, we know. But relationships are about compromise, you know?"

"Yeah, yeah. It's all about give and take."

"And you cannot do all of the taking." Daisy locked her

9

front door and headed into the kitchen. "Care for a glass of lemonade?"

"Yes, please."

Daisy poured a tall glass of homemade lemonade for her brother and one for herself as they took a seat at the kitchen table.

"You know," Daisy began before taking a sip of the lemonade, "you could always come to church with Enrique and me."

"Why?" Sebastian asked before gulping half of his lemonade.

"Single people meet significant others at our church."

Sebastian nearly choked on the remainder of his beverage. "What is with you?" he asked after coughing for a minute.

"What?" Daisy asked innocently.

"Ever since you got married, I can't breathe without you trying to set me up with someone!"

"That's not completely true."

"That's not completely true," Sebastian mimicked. "You're worse than Mom."

"Oh, Mom's trying to set you up too? I must talk with her about this matter."

"No!" Sebastian replied. "Is that all you women like to do in your spare time? Play matchmaker?"

Daisy laughed.

"Well," she began before shrugging and ending with a smile.

Sebastian took the opportunity to change the conversation. "How's your job search going?"

Daisy had a degree in public relations but had not landed a job since graduation from college and getting married, two events that followed each other immediately. "It's going."

"You should check the job ads in the city newspaper."

"Believe me, I have."

"Have you tried applying online?"

"I've tried everything," Daisy said with a sigh.

"Why don't you check marketing companies in Southern California?"

"Like what?"

Sebastian shrugged.

"Hannah told me that she knows people at Boulevard Fashions."

"Oh! Hannah, your best gym buddy?" Daisy replied with interest. "How's she doing? Is she still single?"

Sebastian shook his head. "She and her personal trainer were secretly dating."

Daisy's eyes grew wide. "They got engaged!"

"You guessed it."

"Sweet!" Daisy replied. "Tell Hannah I said congratulations!"

Sebastian rolled his eyes. "Sure."

Daisy's eyes danced, causing Sebastian to grow wary of what his sister was going to say next. "What?"

"Don't drink the water," Daisy advised. "You may be next."

"Not if I can do anything about it."

Daisy sighed. "I'll pray for you."

"Why doesn't anyone believe that a man can be happy *and* a bachelor?" Sebastian asked in frustration.

"Because it's simply not possible," Daisy replied. "God created us for companionship. Just look at our first parents, Adam and Eve."

Sebastian sighed. "I can't argue with you there."

"*See?*" Daisy replied. "Don't worry, SB. When the time is right, God will send you the love of your life."

Sebastian glanced at his watch. It was noon and time for his workout at the gym. "Thanks for all the advice, sis," he said, giving his sister a kiss on her loose, honey-brown curls.

"Anytime, bro," Daisy replied before seeing him to the front door.

Sebastian walked to his Highlander Jeep and waved goodbye to his sister from the driver's seat before driving out of the small neighborhood and onto the main highway.

*Women,* he thought. *Can't live with them, can't live without them.*

*Love Unexpected*

# Chapter 4

*E*smeralda lay curled up in bed, crying silent tears. It was just before noon on Tuesday morning, and she had called in sick. What started earlier in the week as mild symptoms of sinus congestion and a sore throat had hit her full force overnight. She woke up with the worst cough, sore throat, and throbbing headache. To make matters worse, she knew that taking off today would mean that tomorrow she would face a ton of paperwork piled high on her desk.

*Dear God,* Esmeralda prayed, *please cure this cold now. I cannot afford to take time off from work.*

The phone rang.

Esmeralda responded by pulling the blanket over her head.

The phone rang again.

Esmeralda buried herself deeper beneath her silk sheets before realizing that it was not the phone that was ringing, it was the doorbell. After the fifth ring, Esmeralda decided to pull herself out of her bed, don her pastel pink bath robe over her pajamas, and walk bare-footed from her bedroom, through the living room, and into the foyer in order to answer the front door.

"Who is it?" Esmeralda asked.

"Chandra," the person on the other side of the door replied. "I've brought lunch."

"Lunch?" Esmeralda winced at the pain in her throat. *How can I eat when it hurts to swallow?*

Esmeralda opened the door to see a smiling Chandra. "Hey Essie!" she greeted then pouted. "You're not feeling that great, are you?"

"I feel horrible," Esmeralda replied before stepping aside and closing the door behind her.

"I'm sorry you're sick. But no worries. Where's the kitchen?"

"Follow me," Esmeralda replied as she walked through her living room and led Chandra to her kitchen. "What do you mean no worries?"

"I took care of everything."

"Everything?"

"The phone calls, the visitors, the messages, the questions from your colleagues."

"How?"

"Like you said, I'm a good worker."

"Any papers on my desk?"

Chandra shook her head. "Nope."

"Why not?"

"I told everyone to think twice about their questions before asking you and they *listened*!"

Esmeralda laughed then made a face from the pain that surged through her throat.

"Here's some chicken noodle soup from that restaurant you love," Chandra said as she began unloading items from the big brown bag she had carried inside. "And I bought throat spray and cough drops for you."

"Thanks, Chandra," Esmeralda replied with a weak smile. "I appreciate it."

"No problem, boss lady. Let me know if you need anything else, and I'll drop it by your house after work."

"You're going back now?"

"Yes, ma'am," Chandra replied. "See you when you get well."

"Hopefully that will be tomorrow."

"No worries, Essie. I've got your back."

Esmeralda smiled, grateful for such a loyal assistant. After seeing Chandra to the door, Esmeralda plopped down onto her couch, turned on the television to the local news, and drifted off to sleep.

~ * ~

Chandra was driving down the highway with a heavy foot on the accelerator. The music in her Mazda Miata coupe was blaring and she was happy. She planned to return to work before lunch break was over, and it looked like she was going to meet her goal in exactly ten minutes. As Chandra prepared to change lanes for her exit, a car slammed into the passenger's side of her vehicle.

Chandra screamed but managed to maintain enough control to steer the car to the side of the road. The car that hit Chandra spun around and ended on the side of the road, not too far from her car. A panicked Chandra immediately hopped out of her car and inspected it for damages. The entire passenger side of her car was dented.

"Oh no!" Chandra crumpled to the bare cement beside her car and buried her head in her hands.

Meanwhile, the driver who had caused the accident emerged from his Jeep and checked the damages. The entire driver's side of his car was scratched and mildly dented. He was inspecting the damage when he heard crying. He turned around and went to see the lady he had run into. He should have known not to text while driving.

"Hey, lady, I'm so sorry!" he apologized. "Are you okay?"

"No!" Chandra screamed as she struggled to rise to her feet. "Why weren't you looking where you were going?"

"Listen, lady," the man replied as he retrieved his phone from his jean pocket. "Let's not get upset. I'm going to call the cops, and we'll be out of here in an hour."

"An *hour*?" Chandra cried. "I've got be at work in ten minutes!"

The man looked at her. "Well, what do you propose we do?"

Chandra scrambled, pulling out her purse out of her car then running back to the man who had caused the accident. "Give me your name and number and we'll settle this later."

"Fine." The man embodied tall, dark, and handsome. "But I'm going to take your license plate number in case you forget."

"Fine," Chandra replied before pulling out a notepad from her purse and looking over at the man's license plate. She quickly penned his tag numbers and then looked up at his broad six foot frame. "Here." She scribbled her name, tag number, insurance information, and cell number on a separate piece of paper and handed it to him. "That's all the information you'll need for your insurance agent."

"And you're sure that you don't want to call the cops?" the man asked.

"Yes!" a somewhat annoyed Chandra answered. "Now write your contact information on this paper so I can call my insurance company from work."

Wow, this woman was bossy—just like his sister. But he obeyed her order.

After exchanging information, Chandra read the stranger's name out loud. "Sebastian Carter. Why does that sound familiar?"

"I'm a personal trainer for some celebrities," he replied.

"Like who?" Chandra asked before remembering that she had limited time to return to the office. "Oh, never mind! I have to go." She hurried to her car.

"Drive safely, lady!" Sebastian called. He glanced at the paper she gave him. "I mean drive safely, *Chandra*!"

"I *was* driving safely," Chandra called back. "*You* need to look where you're going!"

Sebastian was about to retort but decided not to as Chandra slammed her car door and drove her car on the highway. *What a day,* he thought to himself before returning to his Jeep where he called his insurance company.

*Love Unexpected*

# Chapter 5

Sebastian got out of his car and walked into the floral shop.

After talking with his lawyer about the accident and finding out that it was his fault, which meant that woman he ran into could make him pay for the accident, he decided to resort to some good old-fashioned charm. He would buy her forgiveness with flowers.

What woman could resist a beautiful floral arrangement and a sweet note? He figured that sending the flowers to Chandra's workplace would make her forget all about slapping him with a lawsuit.

*Now I need to find out where she works*, Sebastian thought, pausing before he talked with a florist. He took out his cell phone and dialed her number. After three rings, she answered.

"Chandra McIntire speaking, how may I help you?"

"Chandra!" Sebastian greeted with enthusiasm.

"This is she. Who is this?"

"Sebastian Carter. I ran into you the other day, literally."

"Why are you calling me?"

"I need your work address."

"Why?"

"It's for my insurance agent," Sebastian lied. "He'd like to contact you at work."

"Well then, you'd only need my work number," Chandra replied.

"No. My agent really needs the address of your company too. You know, in case he needs to send his people out there to inspect your car in the parking lot."

"Chandra!" a beautiful yet bossy tone of voice rang loud and clear in the background.

"Hold on," Chandra told Sebastian. "Yes, Essie?"

Sebastian listened in to Chandra's conversation. "Dina and Jon called," the voice said. "You didn't tell me we have a marketing meeting with them today!"

"Essie, I—" Chandra started before remembering she had Sebastian waiting. "Hold on. Sebastian?" Chandra spoke into the phone. "Listen, I've got to go. Our company is called Boulevard Fashions. We're right off of Hollywood Boulevard. Look us up. Bye."

"Chandra, wait! I really need the add—" Sebastian started before realizing the conversation was over.

"Can I help you?" a kind voice inquired.

Sebastian turned to see one of the florists by his side. "Yes," he said. "I'd like to buy a flower arrangement."

*Love Unexpected*

# Chapter 6

*Wednesday afternoon at Boulevard Fashions*

Sebastian drove along the parkway which was lined with beautiful palm trees.

After speaking with Chandra, Sebastian bought a flower arrangement from the florist and decided to personally deliver the bouquet to Chandra. Now all he had to do was to find her office building and he was hoping his new navigator would guide him in the right direction.

"Make a right on Sunset Boulevard," the navigator said, and Sebastian obeyed. Ten minutes later, he pulled into the visitor's parking lot of Boulevard Fashions.

He checked his good looks in the rearview mirror before grabbing the arrangement of yellow roses which the florist told him meant *I'm sorry*. Confidence was on his side as he strolled into the office building's front lobby and headed straight for the receptionist desk.

"Hey," he drawled to the receptionist, "my name's Sebastian Carter. I'm here to see Chandra McIntire."

The receptionist blushed under the gaze of Sebastian's piercing brown eyes.

"Give me one minute," she said as she quickly averted her eyes to the staff directory and picked up the telephone.

"Chandra," she whispered. "A man named Sebastian Carter is here to see you, *and* he's fine!"

Sebastian overheard the receptionist's compliment and grinned. The receptionist hung up the telephone and returned her gaze to Sebastian.

"She said to take the elevator to the fifth floor," the receptionist instructed. "Her office is the tenth cubicle to the right."

Sebastian grinned. The receptionist blushed. He tipped his sunglasses, perched on top of his head, at the receptionist before following her directions.

*Make me pay for the accident?* Sebastian thought as he got into the elevator. *Not after this class act!*

~ \* ~

"Chandra, I—" Esmeralda started then paused.

"Yes, Essie?" Chandra looked up from the pile of papers that were on her desk.

"Who's that?" Esmeralda whispered.

"Who's who?" Chandra asked, getting got out of her chair to see what her boss was gawking at.

The scene before Chandra's eyes was unbelievable. A tall, dark, and handsome man who resembled the famous wrestler Dwayne Johnson, The Rock, walked with great confidence and cast a disarming smile toward her office cubicle. With every step he took, the women who had been about their business swooned. Chandra and Esmeralda did not move as he approached their office area.

"Chandra," the man greeted with an award-winning smile.

"Yes?"

"These are for you," he said, presenting her with the floral arrangement.

Chandra felt a blush threatening to surface.

"Thank you," she said before coming back to her senses. *Wait a minute, I know this man! He ran into me on the highway.*

"Sebastian Carter," she stated plainly.

"You two know each other?" Esmeralda asked.

"Yes. He ran into me on the highway."

"Literally?"

"Yes. And I bet he thinks this Casanova act will keep him from paying for the accident!"

Sebastian's confidence started to deteriorate, and his smile faded. This was not the response he had expected.

"Well, let me tell you something, Mister," Chandra began. "I spoke with my insurance agent this morning and the accident is *your* fault, and *yes*, I am going to charge you for the damages because, unlike you, I am not rich!"

"Chandra," Esmeralda said, giving her employee a look that chastised her for speaking in such a harsh tone of voice.

"Take your flowers," Chandra said, thrusting the beautiful bouquet back into Sebastian's arms. "And leave!"

"Excuse us," Esmeralda said to Sebastian before taking Chandra by the arm. "I need to talk with my assistant before you leave."

A stunned Sebastian simply nodded his head. Esmeralda pulled Chandra into her office cubicle and started talking in a hushed but harsh tone. "What is wrong with you?"

"What is wrong with *me*?" Chandra cried. "I'll tell you what's wrong with me! That man is trying to persuade me not to sue him for damages to my car!"

"Chandra, he did take time to stop by the workplace with a beautiful bouquet! Surely you could at least thank him for his kindness."

"Thank him?" Chandra asked, appalled. "For what? Denting my car beyond repair?"

"Your car can't be *that* damaged."

"Well, it is!"

Esmeralda sighed. "I'm sorry to hear that. But, Chandra, please take the flowers."

Chandra put her hands on her hips and stared at her boss in defiance. Esmeralda copied Chandra's stance. After a forty-second stare down, Chandra gave in. "Fine!" she said before marching out of the office and facing Sebastian.

"Thank you!" she snapped as she snatched the flowers out of his strong hands.

"You may leave now," she added before spinning on her heel and disappearing into her office cubicle.

Esmeralda stepped forward. "I apologize for my assistant. She's having a bad day." She extended her hand. "Esmeralda Rodriguez."

"Sebastian Carter," he replied, shaking her hand.

"Do you always make the girls go crazy over you?"

Sebastian grinned.

Esmeralda smiled back. "I see."

Suddenly Esmeralda's eyes sparkled. She had an idea! Dina said she could help in picking the models for the fashion show, and Sebastian would be perfect. All she had to do was convince Dina, Jon, and Sebastian.

"Sebastian, do you model?" she asked.

"No. I'm a personal trainer."

"Have you ever thought about modeling?"

Sebastian shrugged. "It depends on what the terms of agreement are."

Esmeralda smiled before responding. "Step into my office. I have a business proposal for you."

*Love Unexpected*

# Chapter 7

Chandra stared at the floral arrangement. It was just after seven o'clock and her boss and co-workers had gone home. She was the only one left on the floor.

*Sebastian Carter,* she fumed silently. *Why do you have to be so hot and bring me such beautiful flowers?*

Tears cascaded down Chandra's cheeks. Chandra had always put up a strong, "Ms. Independent" front when it came to love and part of it was due to past hurts.

*In love stories and real life, the guy always gets the girl,* Chandra thought. *Only I'm never the girl the guy gets.*

So to keep her heart from being broken, Chandra acted like she didn't need anyone—even handsome men who took time to bring her flowers.

Naturally, Chandra questioned Sebastian's motives. Given the circumstance of the car accident being his fault, Chandra felt that he wasn't being completely sincere in his gift. Somehow, she had an idea that he didn't want her to slap him with a lawsuit for ruining the passenger side of her car.

Suddenly, a small pink envelope positioned in the center of the bouquet caught Chandra's eye and she picked it out and opened it.

*Dear Chandra,* the note read in fancy handwriting, *Please forgive me for the accident! Perhaps meeting you was not an accident though. Respectfully yours, Sebastian.*

The tears found their way from Chandra's cheeks onto her desk and it wasn't long before she buried her head in her arms on top of her desk and had a good cry.

~ * ~

In his luxurious condo, Sebastian sat at his kitchen table, his plate full of food, yet he could not bring himself to eat. And he knew why—Chandra. He simply could not get the woman out of his mind. Sebastian wasn't used to women being able to resist his good looks and charm, so this situation with Chandra was a first. And to his surprise, he liked the challenge.

*There's something about Chandra,* Sebastian thought as he tried to sort through his feelings for this woman he barely knew. Suddenly, he got an idea. He would call the one woman he knew who could give him unbiased insight into this situation, his sister. Sebastian slipped out of his chair, picked up his cordless phone from the coffee table in the living room, and dialed Daisy's number.

"Daisy," Sebastian said as soon as his sister picked up the telephone. "We need to talk."

"What happened?"

"I think I'm falling in love."

Daisy, who couldn't believe her ears, laughed. "Really? With who?"

"Chandra McIntire."

"Nice, strong name. How did you two meet?"

"Daisy, it's crazy! I ran into Chandra on the highway, and the accident was my fault so I bought her a bouquet of flowers and took it to her workplace and—"

"Wait," Daisy interrupted. "You brought it to her *workplace?* Wow, Sebastian. Why?"

"I figured if I gave her flowers, she wouldn't be mad at me for causing the accident and—"

"Wouldn't make you pay for the damages?" Daisy finished.

"Exactly. So I went to her office and gave her the flowers, but she *rejected* them and told me to take a hike!"

Daisy laughed. "So did you?"

"Did I what?"

"Take a hike?"

"No," Sebastian, who did not appreciate his sister's humor, insisted. "I was about to leave the office when her boss—a lady named Esmeralda—pulled her aside and talked with her. The whole time, I got this weird feeling."

"What kind of feeling?"

"I don't know," Sebastian replied. "It was weird, because nobody's ever rejected me before."

"There's a first time for everything."

"Daisy! Just *listen*! Please!"

"I'm all ears."

"I felt . . . intrigued," Sebastian continued. "This woman is not like any other woman."

"How so?"

"She's feisty, bright, and beautiful."

"Sounds like a real catch," Daisy said before allowing Sebastian to complete his story.

"So when Chandra and her boss returned, she decided to take the flowers, but she quickly returned to her cubicle and didn't come out again."

"And then what happened?"

"Then," Sebastian responded, "her boss pulled me into her office with a business proposal."

"What kind of proposal?"

"Something about needing a male model to headline the fashion week show with Prima and Primo."

"Prima and Primo!" Daisy squealed, immediately recognizing the names of the famous duo. "Well, did you say yes?"

"Yes."

"SB! Do you know who you're dealing with? Prima and Primo are the next Dolce and Gabbana!"

"This is a big deal, huh?"

"The biggest!" Daisy paused. "But back to Chandra. It sounds like you've met the love of your life."

"Now, Daisy, let's not get ahead of ourselves."

"Sometimes love is unexpected."

"Unexpected?"

"Yes, sir. I need to cook dinner before Enrique comes home, SB. Great talking with you. I'm always here if you need advice."

"All right, Daisy," Sebastian replied. "Take care."

He glanced at the clock. It was six o'clock which meant that he had one hour to eat and change into his gym clothes for his scheduled workout with a client. Sebastian poured a glass of juice for himself and slowly poured a separate glass of water.

*I may as well drink the water,* he thought to himself, *because it looks like I've already caught whatever is in it.*

*Love Unexpected*

# Chapter 8

Esmeralda pulled Chandra into her office. "Don't get mad."

"Why?" Chandra asked.

"I've talked with Dina and Jon."

"And . . . "

"They're delighted to know that Sebastian Carter has agreed to spearhead the fashion show each day for fashion week."

Chandra felt a blush creeping upon her cheeks once again. "When was this decided?"

"That fateful day when Sebastian brought you flowers."

"Oh, I see."

"You're not mad?"

"No, why would I be?"

Esmeralda studied her assistant, who was unusually calm after hearing this news, before replying. "Because we will see more of him starting next Monday."

"Monday?"

"The opening show is at noon on Monday—did I send you the memo?"

"I didn't receive a memo, no."

Esmeralda turned to her desktop computer and quickly sent

the memo via e-mail. She swiveled her office chair around to face Chandra. "You have it now."

Chandra returned to her office and sat, staring at the beautiful bouquet she'd received yesterday. A smile tugged at her lips and blossomed into a grin which transformed into laughter.

*Well, what do you know?* Chandra thought. *Maybe meeting Sebastian is part of God's plan for our lives.*

"Chandra?" a voice called.

Chandra moved her gaze from the flowers to her boss.

"Could you go to Clara's Coffee Shop and grab a latte for me?"

"Yes, ma'am," Chandra replied.

"Thanks, sweetie," Esmeralda said. "And after you return, we'll go over the details for Monday with Dina and Jon."

"Yes, ma'am," Chandra said again as she donned her green coat and slipped her purse over her shoulder.

~ * ~

Sebastian's car came to a screeching halt in the parking lot of Clara's Coffee Shop. He had fifteen minutes to grab a salad and bottled water before heading out to meet one of his celebrity clients for a day of personal training in the great outdoors, which for this client, meant running up and down one of California's broadest boardwalks that stretched for miles. Sebastian rushed through the café's door, only to be slowed down by an exceptionally long line of customers awaiting service.

"Great," Sebastian said before turning around to leave.

*Maybe I can make it to the corner Starbucks,* he thought. Sebastian swung the door open and rushed out, only to collide with a young lady of short stature and petite size.

"Watch where you're going!" the young woman exclaimed.

"Hey, I'm so sorry, Miss," Sebastian said as he helped her stand.

"I don't need your help." She pushed him away and dusted off her green coat. As they prepared to move on, their eyes met and they recognized each other.

"This is becoming a habit," Sebastian said as a slow, sheepish smile spread across his face.

Chandra averted her eyes to keep from blushing under the deep stare of Sebastian's coffee brown eyes.

"I'm sorry, Sebastian. Excuse me," she said in a quiet voice.

"Hey, wait," Sebastian said, reaching out to stop Chandra by placing his hand on her arm. Their eyes locked once more.

"The line . . . " He stumbled over his words. "It's kind of long in there."

"That's okay. I have time to spare."

A smile tugged at the corner of his lips. "All right."

A slow smile emerged on Chandra's face. "All right," she echoed.

"I guess I'll see you later. Monday?"

"Monday for the fashion show, yes," Chandra confirmed. "Congratulations on signing the deal."

"Yeah, I'm looking forward to it. The fashion show, I mean."

Chandra nodded then averted her gaze to his hand which was still resting on her arm. Sebastian followed her gaze and became embarrassed. "I better go," he said, removing his hand and placing it into his jean pocket. "Have a good one."

"You too," Chandra replied before disappearing into the café.

Sebastian returned to his car with the broadest smile on his face.

*Love Unexpected*

# Chapter 9

Chandra and Esmeralda sat in front row seats for the Prima and Primo fashion show. The music blared while models got ready backstage. After five minutes, the announcer introduced the models, starting with Sebastian. Upon his appearance on the catwalk, the ladies in the audience went wild. The announcer spoke of Sebastian as if he had modeling for years.

Chandra watched Sebastian work the catwalk and make the hearts of all the ladies in the room melt with his award-winning smile. A small smile started on Chandra's face and reached full bloom as Sebastian singled her out in the crowd and winked.

Cameras began to flash, and Chandra fought off a serious blush.

"He likes you," Esmeralda whispered after Sebastian left the stage.

"What?" Chandra shouted, unable to hear her Esmeralda's voice over the music and applause from the audience.

Esmeralda leaned near to Chandra's ear. "Sebastian likes you and would like to take you out after the show."

"How do you know?"

"It was part of our agreement."

"What?"

"He agreed to do the fashion show only if, one, he was paid and, two, you would go out with him at least once."

Chandra blushed and for the first time felt butterflies in her stomach. While deep in her heart she liked the idea of spending time with Sebastian, she wasn't ready to give into his charms this easily. "I'm not going out with Sebastian."

"Yes, you are."

"Why do you say that?"

"Because I have your car keys," Esmeralda said, retrieving the item from her purse to show Chandra. "You can't go anywhere but out with him."

"That's not fair!"

"Just go out with him this once. And if I'm wrong about him liking you, I will give you a whole day off with paid leave after fashion week is over."

"A *whole day* off?"

"In its entirety."

Chandra silently weighed the outcomes. *What's the worst that could happen?* she thought. *It's only a date, not a lifetime commitment.* "Fine. I'll go."

~ ✳ ~

*Monday evening, at Ristorante Amore on Sunset Boulevard*
Sebastian pulled out a chair for Chandra to sit in.

Chandra thanked him for the kind gesture and took the seat. He sat down, and for a moment Chandra observed the calming ambiance of the restaurant. Cascading water fountains lined the warmly painted walls, and soft music played in the background. Everything from the table cloths to the menus said elegance and romance.

Chandra offered Sebastian a shy smile. The restaurant wasn't the only attractive aspect of the evening. Both she and Sebastian were looking their best, thanks to Dina. Upon learning of the date, Dina insisted that Chandra wear one of the extra dresses and sandals from the show, and Sebastian wore his favorite apparel from the show. The result was a very stylish couple.

"This place is beautiful," Chandra said.

"Yeah," Sebastian agreed with a sheepish grin. "Thank you for agreeing to dine with me."

Chandra blushed. "It's my pleasure."

"So what do you like to eat?" Sebastian asked as he picked up a menu.

"Food," Chandra replied quickly then laughed. "I'm sorry, Sebastian. I mean I like chicken and vegetables."

Sebastian smiled. "I know just what to order for you. May I?"

"Sure," Chandra said with a nervous smile.

She wasn't used to people ordering her food for her, but she promised Esmeralda that she would be on her best behavior and, in Esmeralda's words, "Give the love-struck fella a chance."

The waiter arrived, and Sebastian impressed Chandra by ordering in a fluent Italian tongue. After the waiter left, Chandra leaned across the table. "You speak Italian?"

"Si, signora."

Chandra had a love for the Italian language but was only familiar with a few conversational words and phrases which she learned from reading books.

"Do you?" Sebastian asked, looking into her eyes.

"Do I what?"

"*Parla Italiano?*"

"Me?" Chandra asked. "Speak Italian? Not really. I just know a few words here and there."

"Like what?"

"Well, I know that this restaurant is called *Amore* which means love."

Sebastian laughed.

Chandra frowned. "I don't like people laughing at me."

Sebastian tried to stop laughing before replying. "It's just the way you said it that was funny. Everyone knows that amore means love."

"You'd be surprised as to what people do and do not know."

Sebastian raised an eyebrow.

"There are people," Chandra explained, "without a love for foreign language, who would have trouble figuring out what the word amore means."

Sebastian saw that he was annoying his date, so he quickly changed the topic. "How do you spend your weekends?"

"At home on my computer, checking my e-mail," Chandra admitted. "I go to church, and I jog along the coastline during the day."

Sebastian's eyes lit up and Chandra noticed. "What?"

"I'm a personal trainer for celebrities, and on sunny days I make them jog for miles down the coastline, on the sand or on the boardwalk."

"Sounds like fun."

"We should go jogging sometime," Sebastian suggested. "You know, like, together."

Chandra blushed at the idea of spending more time with him.

"Yeah, we should," she admitted, speaking from her heart instead of her head which said, *No, you're happy jogging alone!*

"Maybe after this fashion week is over, we can meet at the Santa Monica beach. Maybe next Sunday?"

*Is this another date?* Chandra wondered silently. *And why do I want to agree to it? I'm not starting to like this man. Am I?*

"Think about it," Sebastian said, after studying her silence. "And call me."

"I will," Chandra said, speaking from her heart once more.

"*Signor e signora*, your entrée," the waiter said as he placed before them two plates of mixed vegetables and lean chicken cooked to perfection.

"*Grazie*," Sebastian said before turning to Chandra. "Let's eat."

Chandra paused.

"What's wrong?"

"Can we pray?" she asked. "You know, say grace?"

"Yes, of course."

Chandra folded her hands and bowed her head, and Sebastian followed suit. When Chandra was silent, he realized that she wanted him to do the honors.

A nervous Sebastian cleared his throat before quietly praying, "Dear God, thank you for this time spent with Chandra and for this delicious Italian food. Please bless our meal and our company. In Jesus' name I pray, Amen."

When he looked up, Chandra had tears in her eyes.

"What's wrong?" he asked.

"That's was a beautiful prayer," she replied before standing.

"Where are you going?"

"I need to be excused, only for a moment." Chandra walked in the direction of the restrooms.

"Hope I didn't say anything wrong," Sebastian said to himself before beginning to eat.

~ ∗ ~

"He prayed for your company," Esmeralda repeated what Chandra was saying.

It was midnight and Chandra was at home, in her bed. She felt that she needed to talk to someone so she called Esmeralda to talk about the date with Sebastian and how she had become emotional when he thanked God for her company during prayer over the food.

"Yes, he's a really sincere person," Chandra told Esmeralda.

"Well. Are you going to see him again?"

"I don't know." Chandra started to cry. "I don't know what's wrong with me!"

Esmeralda laughed.

"Sweetie, you're falling in love," Esmeralda said. "It's normal to be emotional at first. Don't worry."

*Falling in love?*

"Looks like you won't need next Monday off," Esmeralda mused.

"Yes, I took your advice and found that he really does like me," Chandra admitted.

"And because I so much enjoy being right, I'm going to give you next Monday off anyway so you can rest."

"Are you sure? What about all the work that has to be done?"

"Don't worry. I think I can handle the details for one day."

"All right, thank you, Essie," Chandra said. "I appreciate it."

"You're welcome," Esmeralda replied. "Take care of yourself and don't worry. Once you and Sebastian become official, you'll become more emotionally balanced."

"Official?"

"I have a good feeling about this one, Chandra. Think with your head, but also listen to your heart and you'll be fine."

"Thanks for the advice, Essie."

"No problem, girl," Esmeralda replied. "Good night."

"Good night."

*Love Unexpected*

# Chapter 10

E smeralda called a staff meeting early Tuesday morning with all five of her marketing team members, including her favorite assistant, Chandra. "Good morning to my illustrious marketing team." Esmeralda greeted them with a smile. "I have news for you."

"What is it?" Liz, who was arguably the team's best marketing and PR asset, spoke first.

"First, thank you all for your hard work these past five years and for your outstanding service for the Prima and Primo fashion week," Esmeralda said. "Geraldina and Jonathan were very pleased."

"No problem! Now tell us the news," Lloyd, who liked people to get to the point, insisted.

"Geraldina and Jonathan were so impressed with our team's performance and my leadership, that they made me an offer that was too good to refuse."

"What's that?" Chandra asked.

"Geraldina and Jonathan's Marketing Director has been on maternity leave and has decided to stay at home with her children until they're ready to attend school."

"And?" Liz prompted, sensing there was more to the story.

"And they've invited me to replace Janet at their office in Washington, D.C."

"You're *leaving?*" Chandra inquired with a cry.

"Yes. I am leaving."

"When?" Lloyd asked.

"Two weeks from today."

"What?" everyone on the marketing team exclaimed.

"Yes, I have to go on to greater things, but don't worry. I've recommended to Human Resources a very capable person whom I think can take this company to the next level."

"Who?" Liz asked.

"Chandra."

"Me?" Chandra asked in pure surprise mixed with quiet delight.

"Yes," Esmeralda confirmed. "Chandra, you are an exemplary employee, and I think it's time for you to move up in the ranks," Esmeralda explained. "So I recommended you to HR."

Chandra smiled before replying, "Thanks, Essie! I would love to rise to the occasion if HR chooses me for the job."

Esmeralda smiled. "All right, is everyone happy?"

"How can we be happy when you're leaving?" Liz asked.

"You can be happy," Esmeralda replied, "because you know that under this new leadership, you can continue not only to fly as one of Southern California's best marketing teams, but you can soar to new heights!"

"Spoken like a true leader," Lloyd remarked.

"Group hug!" Esmeralda ordered.

Everyone gathered around Esmeralda and gave each other a big hug.

"Now back to work!" Esmeralda demanded.

Everyone promptly returned to their office cubicles and continued working.

Chandra remained behind. "Essie?"

"Yes, Chandra?"

"Thank you for the recommendation."

"You're welcome."

"I'm going to miss you around here."

Essie gave a sad smile. "I'm going to miss everyone too."

"And I appreciate your role in getting me and Sebastian together."

Esmeralda's eyes twinkled. "So you're a couple now?"

Chandra blushed. "Sort of. I mean, we're going on a second date, and he's totally into me."

"Sounds promising."

Chandra engulfed her boss in a bear hug. "Thanks so much for getting me out of my hard shell, Essie! I wish you all the best."

"I wish you well too, Chandra. Now get back to work."

"Yes, ma'am," Chandra said as she walked toward her cubicle. She paused and faced her boss. "Who knows? You might meet someone back home in D.C."

Esmeralda simply smiled before returning to her office and tackling her to-do list.

*Love Unexpected*

# Epilogue

*Two years later*

Chandra peeked through the windows and gazed down at her guests as they slipped into their seats on the beach-facing terrace. A soft smile graced her face, and her heart warmed as she realized that this was it—she was getting married to someone she never expected to meet, much less fall in love with. She had a peace that made this day even more beautiful than the wedding planner's best efforts.

A gentle knock sounded at her door.

"It's open," Chandra said.

The door eased open, and a familiar face peeked into the room, a face which Chandra recognized easily. "Essie!"

A brilliant smile graced her former boss's face. "Hey, girl." Essie walked into the room. "Are you ready to say 'I do' to the man of your dreams?"

Chandra engulfed Essie in a big hug. "Yes, thanks to your matchmaking, I will!"

Essie smiled. "You look beautiful."

"Thanks, and so do you. How's life in D.C.?"

"D.C. is great. I'm having a great time at work." Esmeralda paused. "But let's catch up after your honeymoon, dear. This time it's all about you. So enjoy it."

Chandra smiled. "We'll have to do lunch whenever Sebastian and I get to visit you on the East Coast."

Essie smiled before reaching into her purse and pulling out a blue hair pin in the shape of a flower. "This is for you," she said. "Something blue."

Chandra gasped. "How did you know? I was just telling my maid of honor that I had my 'Something old, something new, something borrowed' but nothing blue! Oh, Essie, you saved the day!"

Essie laughed. "Happy to help. Now I'm going to go take my seat outside on that beautiful terrace. See you when you walk down the aisle."

Chandra smiled and waved goodbye to Essie as her makeup artist guided her to the chair in front of the mirror so she could apply the final touches to Chandra's look.

~ * ~

An hour later, Sebastian and Chandra had said 'I do' and walked hand-in-hand toward the hotel's luxurious garden area, their wedding photographer in tow while their guests made their way to the hotel's dining hall.

"Is this everything you wanted?" Sebastian asked his wife.

Chandra looked up into his coffee-brown eyes. "More than what I wanted."

"Can't get any better, can it?"

"Yes, it can. We're going to St. Lucia for our honeymoon, remember?"

"Oh, yes, the beautiful island of St. Lucia," Sebastian said before cupping his wife's chin in his hand. "But never as beautiful as you."

Chandra smiled. "I love you, Sebastian."

"I love you too, Chandra."

The couple shared a deep kiss, completely oblivious to the flash of their wedding photographer's camera, because in that moment, all that mattered was this simple truth—they found love, unexpected, and it was beautiful.

# Book Two:

## *The Best Gift*

# *The Best Gift*

# Chapter 1

"Grr." Christina Caballero fussed as she struggled to shimmy into her bridesmaid dress for her younger sister's winter wedding. She'd struggled with weight all her life but was hoping the no carb diet she'd been on would help her be a fit and fabulous bridesmaid. But today she was sad because her diet, which was pure torture to her carb-loving appetite, apparently hadn't worked. Tears formed in Christina's almond-shaped eyes as she realized that this dress was not going to make its way past her expansive hips—and she'd already tried to get into the dress using the over-the-head method.

*I can't be too fat! This dress fit perfectly in August. I couldn't have gained that much weight and inches in only four months.*

There was a knock at the door.

"What?" a frustrated Christina shouted.

"Honey, it's time for dinner," her mother said. "Are you okay?"

"I'm not eating dinner for the next twenty-eight days!"

Christina's sister, Juliette, was getting married to her sweetheart on Sunday, December twenty-eighth, and Christina was determined to look beautiful in her bridesmaid dress. After all, she was the maid of honor.

Christina could hear a quiet chuckle on the other side of the door. She cracked the door open to see her mother, trying and failing horribly to contain her laughter.

"It's not funny. I'm too fat."

"Christina, honey." Mrs. Amanda Caballero tried to reason with her twenty-four-year-old daughter. "You need to have a little fat. You don't want to look anorexic."

Christina gave her a look. "Mom, look at me. I'm *obese*—far from anorexic."

Christina's mom gave a stern look to her grown-up child. "Now, Christina Justine, do not let me hear you speak of yourself in a negative light."

"It's true! My body mass index is off the charts."

"So you're a little chubby. But you can tone that muscle before the wedding."

"How?" Christina asked dryly.

"Merry Christmas!" Mrs. Caballero gave her daughter a card.

"What's this?"

"Open it."

Christina tore the envelope open and read the paper contents. "A two-week guest pass to the gym?"

Amanda nodded. "And if you like going to the gym, I will pay for your first full year of membership."

For the first time that day a smile graced Christina's face.

"Thanks, Mom," she said. "I'm going tomorrow morning before work."

"Good idea," Amanda agreed. "Now let's eat dinner before your younger brother consumes it all."

As if on cue, a boy's voice called from the kitchen. "Mom! Come on! I'm hungry!"

Christina and her mother shared a look and burst out into laughter.

"I'll be there in a minute," Christina told her mom before closing her bedroom door.

She managed to shimmy out of the sapphire blue Vera Wang

dress and quickly donned a pair of jeans and her favorite green sweater.

"I will fit into this dress on December twenty-eight," Christine vowed as she placed the dress in its plastic wrap and hung it inside her closet. "So help me God!"

Christina slipped the guest pass into her purse and hurried to the kitchen to eat dinner before it went cold.

~ * ~

Jordan quietly filed through her little pink address book. "Justin—no. Brian—maybe. Luke—yeah, right."

It was Monday, December first, and Jordan was on her lunch break at work, filing through her phone book, looking for just the right guy to bring home to meet her parents.

"Ruben—hm, haven't heard from him since our break-up, but that's not usual. Maybe I should—"

"What are you doing?" A familiar voice interrupted.

Jordan took one look at Molly Mallet, a colleague she simply did not like, and made a face. "Nothing you'd know about."

"Try me," Molly challenged as she took a seat across the table and began to unpack her lunch.

Jordan studied Molly's face. She was serious. And Jordan did need to talk to someone about it. "My parents gave me an ultimatum: bring a serious beau to Christmas dinner or go home to Sweden for one week, starting December twenty-eighth, to be discovered by my future husband."

"And you're actually looking for a date?" a very surprised Molly voiced. "I'd bring nobody to dinner and be on the first plane flying to Europe!"

"I didn't expect you to understand." Jordan continued to flip through her pink book.

"What's to understand?" Molly challenged. "Obviously your parents have had it with your frivolous dating style and want you to settle down. You've never been serious about your men, so they're giving you an ultimatum—get serious or get lost."

Jordan flashed an angry look at Molly, causing her to laugh. "Relax, Jordan. It's not my fault that you have commitment phobia."

"Whatever," Jordan snapped before standing up, grabbing her purse, and snatching up the apple she had brought for lunch.

"Bye-bye," Molly called after Jordan who was storming furiously out of the employee lounge. "Don't let the door hit you on the way out!"

~ * ~

At a fancy restaurant in northwest Washington, D.C., Joshua Thompson was on one knee, looking up into the midnight blue eyes of the love of his life, Maria Martello. He opened the box containing a four-carat diamond ring and asked her to marry him, fully anticipating a resounding *yes*.

To his surprise and dismay, he received a solid *no*.

Crushed, Joshua wrapped his arms around his girlfriend's waist and pleaded with her to say yes.

"Let me go," Maria Martello whispered aggressively, before taking a quick survey of all the bystanders. "You're making a scene!"

"I can't live without you, Maria. You're my life."

"Well, that's sad," Maria whispered harshly. "And it's the exact reason I'm leaving you."

Maria wriggled free.

"Get a life, Josh. And then maybe true love will find you. Good riddance."

Joshua stood up and tried to run after Maria before being stopped by the maitre d'.

"Sir, you've caused enough reaction from the patrons," he told Joshua in a calm yet stern voice. "You need to leave now."

A heartbroken, devastated Joshua slowly obeyed, dragging his feet as he left the restaurant.

*I can't believe she left me,* he thought as he walked toward the parking lot. *I loved her and thought we'd marry. Now she's gone—out of my life forever. How will I live without her?*

Joshua climbed into his steel-black Jaguar coupe and headed for the Beltway—he needed to drive the entire stretch just to clear his mind.

As Joshua drove, he took a trip down memory lane. He met Maria at church where she was the choir director. It was love at first sight from his point of view. She was perfect with sleek black hair, expressive blue eyes, milky skin, a svelte figure, and the most beautiful voice. Smitten yet shy, Joshua begged Mariska, one of his good friends who went to Maria's church, to introduce him to the woman he knew he would marry. Mariska arranged a blind date for the two and to Joshua's delight, they had an instant connection.

For a while, everything was going great until five months ago when he noticed Maria's deep blue eyes no longer sparkled when she saw him. She started canceling their time together, saying she had to work late. Joshua knew Maria was busy in her career as a music educator for high school students, so he was fine with it until now.

*What went wrong? Is she in love with another man?*

Lost in his thoughts, Joshua didn't realize he'd arrived in his neighborhood until a deer darted across the road. He stepped on his brakes to avoid hitting it. The near miss caused him to become more alert.

*I've got to win her back,* he told himself as he parked in his designated spot and shut off the engine. As he hopped out of his vehicle and walked toward his apartment building, he was silent, but his brain actively plotted ways to woo Maria again.

# The Best Gift

# Chapter 2

Joshua's digital alarm clock beeped for the tenth time in one hour and once again, Joshua blindly pressed the snooze button.

Bright rays of sunlight filtered through the white mini-blinds covering his window. It had to be nine o'clock. An hour late for work already. But who cared? He didn't. Not anymore. He spread his arms across the mattress. What was the point when Maria was gone? He rolled over and placed the pillow over his head. *Why did the woman of my dreams break up with me?*

*Beep! Beep! Beep!*

Just as Joshua was about to hit the snooze button once more, his house phone rang.

"What kind of wakeup call is this?" Joshua shouted as he grudgingly climbed out of his bed and walked to the cordless phone mounted on his bedroom wall. "What is it?" Joshua answered the phone with an attitude.

"Somebody woke up on the wrong side of the bed," the familiar female voice said. "At least you're awake."

"Mariska," Joshua sighed in exasperation. "What do you want?"

"You're lucky it's snowing or you'd have no excuse for being late to work."

"It's snowing?" He walked to his window and opened the blinds. A wintery mix fell so strongly that Joshua could barely see his car in the driveway. *That's an understatement! It's a blizzard out here!*

"Mark is going to fire you if you're not here in one hour," Mariska said. "Just thought I'd let you know."

"Great." Joshua, who knew Mark's leadership style too well, had no doubt Mariska was telling the truth. "Tell Mark I'm stuck in traffic and will be there ASAP."

"Copy that," Mariska said playfully. "Over and out."

Joshua hung up the telephone and began the rush to get ready for work and keep his job.

~ * ~

Jordan sat in the lunch room, using her cell phone to make a personal call.

It was noon, and she was calling the one boyfriend who lavished her with gifts and quality time when they were dating. He was the one man with whom she'd begun to envision herself marrying one day—until she decided she didn't like his haircut and broke up with him.

Desperate times called for desperate measures. He might not call Jordan like the other men, begging her for a second chance, but Jordan was sure he was still into her. After all, who wasn't? Men thought she was irresistible.

"Hello?" The familiar tenor voice sounded over the phone.

A smile graced Jordan's face. "Hey, Ruben," she said. "How are you?"

"Who's this?"

A frown replaced her smile. *He doesn't remember the best five weeks of his life?* "It's Jordan."

"Jordan who?"

"Jordan Mayfield."

"Oh!" Ruben exclaimed. "Jordan!"

"Yeah. What have you been up to?"

"Wedding plans."

"What?"

"I met someone," he said. "She's a beautiful person, and we're getting married."

Jordan became silent, but her mind was racing and shouting. *No! This can't be! He's over me?* "I'm sorry to hear that," she finally said.

"What?"

"I said it's *your loss!*" Jordan shouted before pressing *end* on her cell phone.

"Aw, is poor Jordie having a bad day?"

Jordan didn't have to turn around to see that it was Molly talking. Jordan responded by storming out of the lounge and making a beeline for the bathroom where she locked herself in a stall and cried over Ruben's wedding news.

*Why doesn't it ever work out for me?*

~ * ~

"All right, ladies, move it!"

Christina struggled to keep up with the aerobics instructor. It was her first day at the gym and she was feeling muscles she didn't know she had.

"Give me one, two, three pushups!"

Christina tried her best but failed miserably, falling to the floor in pure exasperation.

"What's this?" the aerobics instructor exclaimed as she hovered over Christina. "Get in workout mode, girl, and smile. You're going to burn fat."

Christina felt her cheeks flush. She was just called out in front of the class of fifty women, all who'd seemed to master the art of the pushup while she failed. Christina fought back tears as she managed to pull herself back into push-up position and revisited the struggle to succeed.

An hour later, Christina was walking painstakingly toward the women's locker room.

"Hey, miss," a masculine voice said.

Christina turned to see a man dressed in the color code for personal trainers at the gym—a blue cotton shirt and black jogging pants.

The man held out a business card. "I saw you struggling in there," he said. "Madeline's not the easiest instructor to work with, but she does get results. I'm Jeff Brown, by the way." He pointed to the business card she'd taken from him. "I'm a personal trainer and would be happy to work with you where you're at and take you to where you want to be in your fitness journey. Plus I'm a lot easier to work with. " He winked. "Promise."

Christina managed a small smile as she looked at the card. He was a certified trainer with a bunch of degree titles behind his name to prove it. "My name is Christina," she said as she extended her right hand. "I appreciate the offer."

"Well, Christina, I hope to hear from you soon," Jeff replied as he gave her a firm handshake. "Now if you'll excuse me, I have a client to meet."

Christina stepped out of his way, her eyes followed him for a moment, then lowered to study his business card. He seemed like the real deal and Lord knows she could not survive another one of Madeline's exercise classes. Granted, she still had a bridesmaid dress to fit into. She resolved to call him that night.

*The Best Gift*

# Chapter 3

Memories of good times with Maria played on the movie screen of Joshua's mind. So lost was he in memories that he did not hear anything being said by his boss and colleagues at their midday meeting.

*What's the meaning of all this?* Joshua's thoughts whirled in his head. *My life revolved around Maria. Now it's like I don't know what to do without her.*

"Earth to Josh," a voice said. "Earth to Joshua," it repeated, this time with more force.

"You can't reach him, boss," Mariska said. "He's far, far away."

Joshua snapped out of it.

"The meeting's over," Mark said. "Is there something you'd like to tell me?"

"No, sir," Joshua said as he gathered his notebook and pen and stood to leave the conference room.

He returned to his cubicle where he worked as a feature story writer for Metropolitan Weddings Magazine. Mariska followed him. "Hey, Josh."

"Go away," he mumbled as he turned on his computer screen.

"Not until you tell me what's wrong."

Joshua gave Mariska one long look.

"Oh, wow," she said. "She didn't."

Joshua nodded.

"Wow," Mariska said. "You mean to tell me that there's actually a woman out there in the world who *can resist* your good looks and charm?"

Joshua buried his head in his hands.

"I'm so sorry, Josh," Mariska said with sympathy. "What happened?"

Joshua shook his head and waved his hand. "She broke up with me at the Brio restaurant in Bethesda," Joshua said. "Something about how it's sad that she's my life and how I need to get a life before true love is able to find me."

Mariska chuckled.

"It's not funny."

"Sweetie, all she's saying is that you were getting too wrapped up in her life. Women need space to breathe too, you know. You probably let your world revolve around her, and she felt like she was being smothered. That's all."

"What are you saying?"

"I'm saying all you have to do is get a life and she'll come back to you. Trust me."

"What do you women mean by get a life?"

Mariska paused before answering. "Well, Josh, you can be kind of . . . conceited, arrogant, self-centered—"

"Do proceed!" Joshua mocked. "You're great for my ego."

"Egotistic!" Mariska cried. "That's the word to describe you."

"Go away. You're not helping."

"Oh, but I am. Listen," she said. "Since it is the Christmas season, I will help you."

"How nice of you," Joshua said dryly.

"Well, if you don't want my help I have plenty of other things to do."

"How can you help me?"

Mariska handed a church bulletin to Joshua.

"What's this?"

"Exactly," Mariska said. "When's the last time you went to church, Josh?"

"Christmas Day, two years ago—that's when I met Maria. She was directing the children's choir."

"Love at first sight, right?"

Joshua nodded.

"That's nice. But here's my point. Before you commit a lifetime to that special someone, you really need to know yourself and what you want in life. And, most importantly, you need to have a closer walk with God."

"What are you saying?"

"I am saying that God created you and He knows what you need. And if what you need is Maria, he will bring you two together. But if He knows that you need to first better understand His character and His divine will for your life, then that's what's going to happen."

"You make it sound like I don't know God."

"I'm not saying that," Mariska countered. "I'm saying that you need to nurture your spiritual life because really only God deserves to be the center of your world—not Maria, not your family, not your friends. Only God can carry you through the troubles of the world. He loves you, Josh, and He knows and *wants* what is best for you."

"Thanks for the sermon," Josh noted. "But what's the church bulletin for?"

"I want you to visit my church this weekend."

Joshua sighed. "I don't know, Mari."

Mariska rested a hand on Joshua's shoulder. "Once you make more time for God in your life, you can make your heart His home."

"What?" a confused Joshua asked.

"Just be at church this Sabbath," Mariska said. "And say your prayers tonight. God will help you. You've just got to know and trust Him."

"Thanks," Joshua said. "I think."

*What's she saying?* Joshua thought as he placed the bulletin in his briefcase. *I have a good relationship with you God, right? Right?*

*The Best Gift*

# Chapter 4

C hristina drove into the parking lot of the beautiful mansion overlooking the National Harbor in southern Maryland. She worked as a photojournalist for Style Mode Magazine, and today her assignment was to cover the wedding of an important political figure.

"Wow," Christina said as she parked her car and the fairy-tale scenery began to sink in. "They must be rich."

Christina lived off an average salary for a photojournalist, and she was sure that unless she married a rich man, she'd never be able to afford a lavish wedding. Quietly, she gathered her purse, camera equipment, and car keys. She shut the door and began to walk up the beautiful, flower-bush-bordered walkway toward the mansion.

Before Christina could ring the doorbell, the door swung open, and a man of average height and fine apparel greeted her. "Hello. You must be from the magazine."

Christina smiled and extended her right hand. "I'm Christina Caballero, and I am the wedding photographer for the soon-to-be Mr. and Mrs. Roberts."

A wide smile graced the man's somewhat pudgy face.

"Greetings, Ms. Caballero!" He stepped aside. "I am Franz, the butler. Please, do come in."

"Thank you," Christina returned as she entered the marble-floored foyer.

"Now the future Mr. and Mrs. Roberts would be pleased to meet you, only they have not yet arrived."

Christina followed him into what looked like a parlor room straight out of a Jane Austen book. Franz faced her. "Why don't you have a seat while you wait?"

Grateful to have time to rest, Christina obliged.

"And would you fancy some green tea?"

Christina shook her head. "No, thank you, I just ate breakfast."

"Very well," Franz said as he handed her a tiny bell. "I will be in the kitchen. Ring if you need me."

Christina smiled, loving the service. "Thank you." After he left, she settled into the cushioned single chair and resisted the urge to kick off her shoes.

*I'm so on assignment,* Christina reminded herself silently. *But I'd love to take a nap right now.*

Christina, who had been on the road since four o'clock that morning, rested her head on the top of the chair and closed her eyes.

~ \* ~

"Sleeping beauty," a playful voice gently beckoned a sleepy Christina to open her eyes. "Wake up."

As Christina's eyes came into focus, she gasped. She'd fallen asleep on the job! How unprofessional. "What time is it?" she asked the handsome stranger.

The man smiled. "Eight o'clock. Franz tells me you're the photojournalist from the magazine."

"Yes, I am." She gathered her camera equipment from the floor and stood. "I am so sorry. I didn't mean to fall asleep, but the parlor is so cozy and soothing, and after being on the road for hours, I guess I needed a nap. I just didn't mean to take it until I returned home."

The man laughed. "It's no problem." He extended his hand. "My name is Eric Hazelton."

"Nice to meet you, Eric. I'm Christina," she said as she returned the handshake. She tilted her head to the right. "You know, you look a lot like—"

"Erica?"

"Yes."

"I'm the bride's brother," he said with a dazzling smile.

Christina blushed. *Erica never told me her brother was so cute!* "That's great. So are you one of the groomsmen?"

"I'm the groom's best man," Eric said. "We were buddies during our college years, and I introduced him to my sister, even though I usually protect her from my friends since she's younger."

"What made Bryant Roberts different from the others?"

"Simple," Eric said. "He's the only one of my friends who understands what Erica wants."

"What do you mean?"

"Women are complicated, right?"

"Yeah, we can be."

"Bryant sees beyond the complexities of my sister and he has a way of warming her heart, even when he's not around."

Christina blushed, wishing she could meet someone who would have that same effect on her someday.

"He treats her with deep admiration and respect," Eric added. "And he's my best friend, and my sister deserves the very best. So needless to say, I'm very pleased that she chose Bryant."

"How sweet."

"Why don't I lead you out to the garden?" he proposed. "The bridal party will be here any minute, and it would be the best place to take pictures before the wedding at noon."

"That would be wonderful," Christina agreed. "Thank you for your assistance."

"It's my pleasure," Eric said as he held open the French doors which lead into the hallway.

*She's beautiful,* he thought as he led her to the garden. Would she agree to a lunch date? It'd be nice get to know her better.

"Here we are," he said as he led her onto the terrace.

"Such beautiful scenery!" Christina cried. She enjoyed it for a moment before going to work.

Eric watched her. He loved how her eyes lit up when she saw the garden, and he adored the zest in her approach to capturing the scenes of life by which she was surrounded.

Franz interrupted Eric's thoughts. "She's a nice girl, eh?"

"Very nice," Eric agreed. "Hey, Franz, can you do a favor for me?"

"It depends on what the favor is."

"It involves asking Christina on a date."

~ * ~

Several hours had passed, and Christina's feet ached. But her heart was happy because she'd managed to take beautiful pictures from a wide variety of angles and believed her editor would be very pleased with her work. Now standing before her open trunk, she gently packed her camera equipment inside. As she slipped inside her car, a very tired Christina glanced at her watch and wishfully pondered having a chauffeur to drive her back to her home in northern Maryland.

"Christina!" a familiar voice called just as she started the car. She glanced in the rearview mirror. Eric was running toward her car.

Christina frowned. *Did I forget something?*

"You did such a great job with the wedding," Eric said as he approached her car. "I wanted to exchange business cards with you."

He handed her a card, and she retrieved one from her purse. "Sure."

"It's been a pleasure doing business with you," Eric said. "Erica and all of us really look forward to seeing the pictures."

She managed to smile. "Thank you, Eric. It's been a pleasure working for your sister."

"Drive safe!" Eric said, wishing she were staying, if only for five more minutes. *I enjoy her company,* he thought. *At least I have her contact information. I hope she has time for a lunch date.*

"Bye now," Christina said as she placed the car into reverse.

"Oh yeah, right!" Eric said as he stepped back from the car. "Goodbye." *And I hope to see you soon.*

*The Best Gift*

# Chapter 5

"Mom, I don't want to hear it!" Jordan shouted.

"Well, I'm going to tell you anyway." Mrs. Rebecca Mayfield followed her daughter from the kitchen into the living room. "You are twenty-five years old. When I was your age, I was married and, soon after, pregnant with you."

"Why does it matter?"

"It matters because I do not want to see my daughter, the bachelorette, become an old maid."

"Mother, I am only twenty-five years old. Relax."

"No! I will not relax. If you do not bring a serious beau to dinner this Christmas Day, then you're spending the remainder of your vacation at Aunt Ana's guesthouse in Sweden where you can meet a nice Swedish man who you'll fall in love with and marry."

"Why marry?" Jordan countered. "I plan to elope!"

"You are a rebel!"

"Oh, now I'm a rebel," Jordan said. "What else am I? Just go through the list!"

"Ladies, calm down."

Jordan and her mother spun to see Mr. David Mayfield—Jordan's dad—enter the room.

"Your daughter," Rebecca began, "plans to elope!"

"Well, at least she's getting married," David returned. "That is what you've wanted for her since she was born, right?"

"Thank you, Dad," Jordan said. "I thought I was the only one feeling this pressure to marry."

"Do what you please," Rebecca said. "But my plan of action still stands. Christmas dinner, my dear child, is your last chance to get serious about your love life."

"My love life?" Jordan objected. "Why with all you've been saying, I didn't know *my* love life belonged to *me*!"

"Don't you dare raise your voice to me," Rebecca countered.

"Well, how dare you tell me, a full-grown *adult*, what to do?"

Rebecca turned to her husband. "You see? See how she treats me?"

"I think the true issue is how *you* treat *me*!"

"Now, ladies—" David started.

But his plea for peace fell on deaf ears—both Jordan and her mother had exited the room, going separate ways and leaving David by himself in the living room.

~ * ~

Jordan lay across her bed, soaking her pillow with tears.

"It's not fair," she sobbed. "Why can't my mom just let me grow up the way I want to?"

Jordan's golden brown, Pomeranian puppy walked to her, and she picked him up, a smile gracing her face for the first time that day. She sat up cross-legged on her bed, cushioning her pet in her lap. "You always listen to me, Fluffy," she said as she began to brush her dog's hair. "Why can't Mom just *listen* to me?"

Jordan wiped tears from her eyes. "It's not like I don't want to get married. It's just that I haven't found the right one yet. You understand that, don't you, Mr. Fluffy?"

*Woof! Woof!*

Jordan laughed. "Dogs truly are man's best friend."

61

The phone rang, causing Jordan to return Fluffy to the floor and search for her cell phone. "Where did I put that thing?"

She jumped off of her bed and hurried to her closet where she kept her pink leather purse. After dumping all its contents onto her bed, she finally found her phone and picked it up.

"Hello?"

"Hey, Jordan baby," a familiar voice greeted.

"Brian?"

"Yes, who else calls you Jordan baby, and do I need to beat them up?"

Jordan, who was automatically adjusting her hair in her mirror, laughed. "Only you call me that, sweetie. Don't worry."

"I'm in town for the holidays." Brian was a senior medical student at a university in Southern California. "Why don't we meet at our favorite place?"

Jordan frowned. She'd forgotten which one was Brian's.

"Starbucks . . . "

"Oh!" Jordan smiled at her reflection, finding it hard to believe that she'd been crying earlier. "I'd be delighted to meet you at Starbucks."

"Good, see you in twenty minutes."

"Right back at you," Jordan said. She ended the call. "All right, Fluffy. Go bye-bye. Mommy has to dress up."

Jordan let her dog out of her room and quickly prepared for her date with one of her favorite ex-boyfriends. *If he's still single,* Jordan thought, remembering how many girls were always after Brian, *maybe he'll agree to be my Christmas dinner date. I guess I still love him, and I'm sure he's not over me yet so maybe Mom will think we're serious and she'll finally stop pressuring me.*

*The Best Gift*

# Chapter 6

"What am I doing here?" Joshua asked beneath his breath.

It was the first Saturday of December, and he had just walked into the lobby of the Stonehenge Seventh-day Adventist Church in Newfoundland, Maryland. Joshua admired the beauty of the architecture, but apart from that, he doubted anything else about the day would be beautiful.

He glanced at his watch. Ten o'clock. According to the church bulletin Mariska had given him, Sabbath School started at ten and the service began at eleven, but there was no sight of Mariska who said she'd meet him in the lobby at ten.

*Maybe I should leave.* Just as Joshua placed his hand on the door to leave, a familiar voice called him.

"Happy Sabbath, Josh."

He turned to face Mariska who enveloped him in a welcoming hug.

"I'm sorry that you wanted to leave." After five years of working together, Mariska knew him pretty well. "But you're going to be happy you stayed."

"I am?"

"Yes," Mariska said with a smile. "Follow me."

She led him up a flight of stairs and into a meeting room filled with young adults.

"They've got a Sabbath School targeted for our age group," Mariska whispered as they entered the room. "Let's find a seat. You're going to love what they have to say. You brought your Bible, right?"

"No." He'd known he was forgetting something. "I didn't."

"No worries, I'll pick up one for you," Mariska said as she picked up a Bible from a shelf and handed it to him.

"Thanks." He accepted the Bible and took a seat next to Mariska.

"Happy Sabbath, Mariska," Kristy, the eldest young adult leader, greeted. "I see we have a visitor."

"Yes." Mariska smiled, placing a hand on Joshua's arm. "We do. His name is Joshua."

Kristy beamed. "Happy Sabbath, Joshua, and welcome to our young adult Sabbath School. I'm Kristy Evans, and I'll be your presenter today."

"Sounds great," Joshua said. "Nice to meet you, Kristy."

Kristy smiled then returned her attention to her friends and Sabbath School members. "Today we're talking about spiritual gifts," Kristy began, opening her Bible. "I'd like everyone to turn to the book of 1 Corinthians. Now the apostle Paul wrote to the Corinthian church concerning spiritual gifts and he said . . . "

Joshua grew quiet as he read through the Bible with his new peers. *This isn't too bad,* he thought. *Maybe I should return next week.*

～ ✳ ～

Christina was busy downloading the photos from the Roberts' wedding onto her computer, so busy that she didn't realize someone had approached her office cubicle until they cleared their throat. "Excuse me, are you Christina Caballero?"

Christina swiveled in her chair and nearly jumped in surprise. The owner of the voice was a delivery boy whose nametag said he was from 1-800-Flowers, and he cradled the most beautiful bouquet of pink roses and baby's breath in his arms.

"Hi," she said. "I wasn't expecting you."

The delivery boy gently placed the bouquet on Christina's desk. She turned her attention to the floral arrangement. "And I definitely was not expecting these!"

"This is for you," the delivery boy said, handing Christina a greeting-card sized envelope. He took out a digital camera. "I have special orders to take a picture of you as you open the card."

"Okay," Christina said. "May I ask who these are from?"

"Special orders say I cannot tell you."

"All right." Christina laughed. "I guess I can follow special orders from a complete stranger."

Quietly, Christina began to open the envelope. Rose petals cascaded to the floor.

The camera flashed repeatedly.

Christina laughed. "Who sent this?"

"I think you're supposed to read the card, ma'am."

*Dear Christina,* the neatly penned words read. *Roses are red, violets are blue . . . I am delighted to have met and been the subject of a beautiful wedding photographer like you. If this sentiment is the same for you, would you please agree to do lunch with me this Friday at noon? Sincerely, Eric Hazelton.*

"Friday at noon?" Christina voiced aloud then turned to the delivery boy and smiled. "Have a good day, and thank you for following your special orders. I appreciate your time."

"It's all part of my job, ma'am," the young man said as he packed away the camera. "You're a lucky lady."

*I must be,* Christina thought. *I truly must be.*

~ \* ~

Jordan waltzed into the office with a broad grin on her face. Memories of her date with Brian and their conversation replayed in her mind.

"So, your mom still wants you to marry ASAP, huh?"

"Yes," Jordan admitted, grateful for Brian's honesty and intuition. "It's impossible to please her. She won't be happy until I'm wearing a wedding ring and bringing my husband and her grandchildren to dinner."

"Jordie, baby, you know that your mom loves you, right?"

"Sometimes, I think she loves the idea of me marrying and moving out of the house more than she loves me."

"Don't believe that lie."

"Well then why is she always pressuring me to find 'The One'? Why can't I travel the world, have fun with my money, you know? Grow into who I'm meant to be and then decide to settle down. I like playing the field. I don't want to commit to anyone right now."

"Have you tried telling your mom?"

"Telling her what?"

"Everything you've just told me."

"No! She won't listen to me unless what I have to say starts with 'I got engaged!'"

"Well, then," Brian said, "will you marry me?"

"What?"

"I said, will you marry me?"

"Stop playing with me."

Brian got down on one knee and took out what looked like a ring case. He opened it, and inside was a lollipop ring. A wide grin stretched across Brian's face and Jordan laughed.

"Sure, Brian, I will marry you. Thank you for the lovely ring."

Brian slipped the candy ring onto Jordan's finger and returned to his chair. "I thought you'd like that idea."

"Not as much as my mom would." Jordan tasted the candy ring. "Mm grape. My favorite flavor."

"Well, if you need me, I'm here."

"Since you mentioned that," Jordan said slowly, "my mom's hosting our annual Christmas dinner in a few weeks. Would you be my date?"

"Gladly," Brian said. "Now what's the real deal?"

Jordan quickly explained her case to Brian.

"You're passing up a trip to Sweden?"

Jordan paused. Molly had given her the same response as Brian.

"Yes, I am. And if you play along well at dinner, I can go to Aruba instead."

"Why not Sweden?"

"I visit Aunt Ana every other summer at her old farmhouse in the countryside. Trust me, if my future husband was a residential Swede, I would have met him by now."

"All right, I'm in."

"All right," Jordan echoed with a smile.

"And I have one condition," Brian said.

"What's that?"

"What would you say if I asked you to marry me for real one day?"

Jordan paused. "Why?"

Brian shrugged. "Just wondering."

"Some things are better left to the imagination."

Brian had shrugged once more. "Hey, it could happen."

Molly's voice woke Jordan from her memory. "Somebody woke up on the *right* side of the bed this morning!"

Jordan continued walking toward her own cubicle. "Good morning, Molly. How are you today?"

Molly hopped out of her chair and followed Jordan into her office space. "Okay," she said once Jordan was seated. "Who are you, and what have you done with the real Jordan Mayfield who hates me?"

"Me, hate you?" Jordan turned her computer on and filed through her inbox. "I have no idea what you're speaking of."

Molly stared at Jordan for a good moment, trying to analyze her, and when she couldn't figure it out, she threw her hands up in the air and left.

The smile never left Jordan's face as she went through her day. It was almost as if she knew the tide was changing for her. She didn't know what it meant, but she had a feeling it meant something spectacular.

*The Best Gift*

# Chapter 7

*J*oshua walked to the café next to his office building with his two-week-old, leather-bound Bible clasped in his hand. Ever since he'd visited Mariska's church and participated in the young adult Sabbath School, his interest in reading God's Word ignited. Now he read the Bible every spare moment he found. Lunch time was the perfect opportunity to steal away from the office, buy something good to eat, and replenish his spiritual food supply.

"Good afternoon, Josh," a friendly voice greeted.

Joshua smiled at Julie who had become his personal waitress ever since she saw him studying the Bible in a corner of the café.

"What chapter are you reading today?" she asked as she poured orange juice for him.

"I'm reading the book of Job."

"Ooh, what's that about?"

"A man who lost it all. By the end of the story, God restored him and blessed his life abundantly."

"Sounds interesting," Julie said as she whipped out her notepad. "May I take your order?"

"Yes. The regular, please."

Julie nodded before leaving for the kitchen to place his order of a tuna fish sandwich and an apple. Meanwhile, Joshua gently laid his Bible on the table and opened the holy book to the final two chapters of Job.

He was deep in God's Word when a glint of silver caught his eye. He looked up to see a familiar sparkly silver purse, and his heart warmed when he recognized the owner of the purse—Maria Martello.

*What's she doing here?* he thought then remembered that she was in town for a few days.

*Should I talk to her?* As he began to stand, Maria caught his eye and, to his surprise, smiled and waved. Joshua motioned for her to have a seat at his table. Maria simply smiled, pointed to her watch, and shook her head.

"Here's your order, Josh." Julie set his food in front of him.

"Thank you." He settled into his chair and cast one more look in Maria's direction, only to see that she was leaving the café.

Joshua was determined to give Maria the space she needed. After studying the Bible, he was realizing how God's thoughts were not like man's musings and how God's ways were not likened to his own. As the days progressed without being by the side of his ex, Josh only grew more confident that if he and Maria were meant to be together, God would work it out. All Joshua needed to do was to stay in tune with the Creator of the Universe.

*Dear God,* he prayed, *please bless this food, and please bless Maria. In Jesus' name I pray, Amen.*

⁓ ✱ ⁓

Christina fixed her hair while looking in her rearview mirror for the fifth time in five minutes.

*I really should just go into the restaurant and wait,* she thought. *It's safer than staying here in my car.*

It was the second Friday of December. Christina was following through on her promise to talk over lunch with Eric Hazelton, and for whatever the reason, it felt like there were butterflies in her stomach.

*Oh no, I'm not falling for him, am I? I barely know him.*

After sending up a quick prayer for God to quiet her nerves, Christina gathered her wits and her purse and climbed out of her car. She entered the restaurant with the most confident gait she could muster.

"Table for one?" the receptionist inquired.

"No. I'm waiting for a friend."

"She's with me."

She turned to see that Eric had been seated in the waiting area on one of the leather couches. He now stood his full stature and gave her that famous, dazzling smile—the same smile that made the butterflies in her stomach perform somersaults. Christina placed a hand over her stomach and extended her right hand to Eric for a handshake. Eric took her hand in his and pulled her into a hug.

"You look amazing," he said, causing Christina to blush.

"So do you," Christina, who wasn't used to public displays of affection, returned the compliment before distancing herself from her lunch date.

"A table for two please," Eric told the receptionist.

"Very well." The woman picked up two menus and cradled them in her arms. "Follow me."

As the waitress placed the menus onto the table, Eric held out a chair for Christina who quietly obliged. They sat and smiled at each other.

"Good afternoon," a friendly voice greeted, causing both Eric and Christina to stop staring at each other and focus on the source of the greeting—a petite woman with carrot-red hair, green eyes, and a timid smile.

"I'm Carina," she explained. "I will be your waitress for today. Can I get you anything?"

"Sparkling water with lemon," Eric and Christina replied in unison, causing a giggle from Carina.

"You two are cute," she said. "How long have you been married?"

"Married?" Christina squeaked.

Eric suppressed his urge to laugh. His eyes twinkled. "We're not married. She just agreed to share lunch with me."

Carina turned a deep shade of crimson. "Oh, I'm sorry."

"It's not a problem. We'll be ready to order in about five minutes."

Carina left.

Christina had trouble looking into Eric's twinkling brown eyes. "I'm so sorry," she finally said.

"Why are you sorry?"

"I don't know why she thought we were married."

"Maybe because we spoke at the same time, about the same order," Eric reasoned. "So, tell me about yourself."

"Well," Christina began, "I am a photojournalist for Style Mode Magazine."

"And what do you do for fun?"

Christina paused then smiled. "Watch romantic comedies."

Eric laughed. "What else do you do?"

She shrugged. "I'm not very adventurous."

Eric nodded.

"Tell me about yourself."

"Well, I'm from a long line of prominent politicians, but I have no love for the political world. My dream is to be a pilot."

"Really?"

Eric nodded. "I'm going to flight school in January."

"Are you scared?"

"No, why would I be scared of the friendly skies?"

Christina laughed, and the ice was broken. The new friends shared stories from their lives over sparkling water and, later, a meal for two.

*The Best Gift*

# Chapter 8

*I*n his living room Joshua sat on his white leather couch with his Bible propped open upon his lap. Today, he was studying the book of Revelation, and for the first time in three weeks, he felt at peace.

*It must be a church-related effect,* Joshua thought. *I really like going to Mariska's church, and fellowship with the congregation does something to me—a good something.*

Joshua took comfort in the promises found within God's Word, and that good *something* stirred within him—a desire to share everything he was learning with everyone he met, starting with Julie, his friend from the café.

His mind went back to the conversation he'd had with her during his lunch break on Friday.

"What book of that famous life-changing book are you reading today, Josh?" she'd asked as she poured a glass of orange juice for him.

"Proverbs," he replied.

"What's God telling you?" Julie, who had become genuinely interested in Joshua's transforming character, inquired.

Joshua turned to the third chapter of Proverbs and read verses five and six aloud. "Trust in the Lord with all your heart; and lean not on your own understanding. In all your ways acknowledge Him, and He shall direct you paths."

"You mean that God has all the answers to my questions?"

Joshua nodded. "God knew us before we knew ourselves. He is the Creator of the universe, this earth, and every human being you see in this café and in the world. He loves us, and He's coming again to take us home."

"When is he returning? 'Cause some days it's like, 'Stop the world, I want to get off!' You know?"

To his surprise Joshua had a ready response. "The Bible says that no man knows the time or the hour of Christ's second coming. Only God knows and for good reason."

"Yeah, I guess." Julie was thinking deeply. "I mean, if everyone knew when God was returning, they'd do whatever they wanted and wait until the very last moment to clean up their act. From what you've been telling me, God doesn't like lukewarm Christianity."

It was then and there that a bright idea popped into Joshua's head. "You should come to church with me this Saturday."

Julie's eyes grew a bit wide. "Saturday? I have plans."

"But what if God has a plan for your life, and He's waiting to reveal it to you?"

Julie paused. "You're right," she said. "I can cancel my plans. I was just going to the mall with my sister."

"Bring her too."

Julie shook her head. "She hasn't wanted anything to do with church since her fiancé died."

"That's all the more reason to bring her," he insisted. "God wants to meet you both where you're at in life. The best way to find out how much He loves you is to first believe in Him and the gift of salvation sent through His Son, and then fellowship with the members of the body of Christ. The people who believe in God are the church, and we all need each other."

"Wow," Julie said. "Sounds like I need to go to this church of yours."

Joshua nodded. "You should."

~ ✳ ~

On Saturday, Joshua was getting ready for church, expecting Julie was going with him. The ringing telephone interrupted his morning routine of studying the Bible and fixing breakfast.

He picked up the cordless phone from its mount on the wall. "Good morning, Joshua speaking."

"Josh, it's Julie."

He glanced at his watch. It was eight o'clock, and he'd promised Julie he'd pick her up for church before nine o'clock.

"Julie, hi! I'll be there to pick you up shortly so we can go to church."

"I won't be there," Julie said.

"Why?"

"It's my sister." Julie began to cry.

Joshua grew worried. "What's wrong?"

"She's been depressed ever since her fiancé died a few months ago, and we thought she was getting better, but today she had a nervous breakdown." Julie sobbed. "We're at the hospital."

"I'll be there," he said.

He picked up his Bible, grabbed his wallet and car keys, and hurried out of his house and to his car. As he started the ignition, he hooked up his Bluetooth to his ear and called Mariska.

"Happy Sabbath, Josh," Mariska said. "You're awake early. Are you coming to church?"

"I may not be there today."

"Why not? What's wrong?"

"My friend Julie's sister is in the hospital. She's really sick. Please have the congregation pray for her."

"Is everything okay?" Mariska asked before adding, "I'll relay your request to our pastor and be sure that we'll pray for Julie's sister."

"Thanks, Mariska," Joshua said. "You're the best."

"Drive safe, and call me when you return home."

"I will," he said. "Goodbye."

Now Joshua was on the Beltway, going full speed toward the hospital exit.

*Dear God,* he prayed, *please help me to know what to say. May Julie's sister and family feel the warmth of Your love and support of Your care.*

# *The Best Gift*

# Chapter 9

Jordan smiled at her reflection in her vanity mirror. She'd just returned home from another date with Brian and she'd never been happier. Ever since he'd learned of her plight, he'd spent more time with her, making both Jordan and her mother very happy.

Jordan sighed. *If only this wasn't short of a charade.*

While Jordan and Brian were naturally good friends, she knew that he was spending so much time with her as part of her proposed plan to help her mother see that she had a serious beau and would not need to go to Sweden.

*Too bad Brian won't propose to me for real,* she thought as a silly smile graced her face. *Because I'd marry him in a heartbeat... I think.*

Jordan laughed off her nervousness.

It was Christmas Day, and she was looking forward to dinner with her parents and Brian. But after spending so much time with him over the past two weeks, she could feel her old feelings for him resurfacing. Visions of beautiful wedding bouquets danced in her head along with the sound of wedding bells.

*What's happening to me?* Jordan thought as she studied her reflection in the mirror. *I look the same, but I feel different. I feel like ... like I'm in love.*

~ * ~

*(Christmas dinner with the Mayfield family)*

Brian stood outside of the Mayfield residence with a beautiful bouquet of red roses clutched in his shaking hands.

*Why am I so jittery?* he wondered then remembered how he was when he first started dating Jordan—before the breakup. *It's the Jordan effect.*

*Dear God,* he prayed, *help me not be so nervous, and please get us both through this dinner.*

Just as he reached out to ring the doorbell, the door swung open and a radiant Mrs. Mayfield greeted Brian with a hug.

"Hello, my future son-in-law," she greeted enthusiastically. "Merry Christmas."

*Future son-in-law? What did Jordan tell her mother? And what have I gotten myself into?*

"Becca, don't scare the boy," Mr. Mayfield said. His words were like music to Brian's ears. "Come in," he told Brian. "Jordan will be down in a minute."

"Oh, yes, please come in." Rebecca took the roses out of Brian's shaky grasp. "Are these for Jordan?"

Brian nodded. "Yes, ma'am."

Rebecca touched Brian's arm. "Please, don't be so formal. Call me Mom."

"Rebecca—," Mr. Mayfield started.

"Oh, I know, I know," Rebecca said to her husband before returning her attention to Brian. "I'm just so happy that Jordan's finally serious about a man."

Brian gulped. "May I use the bathroom?" he managed to ask.

"Sure, sweetie. You remember where it is, right?"

Brian nodded and made a hasty exit.

Meanwhile, Jordan was doing the final fix to her makeup. She smiled at her reflection in the powder room mirror and turned around and opened the door. Jordan jumped in surprise at the sight before her—Brian stood there with a look of pure panic over his face.

Jordan tried not to laugh. "Brian, Merry Christmas! What's wrong?"

"Your mom thinks we're getting married. She told me to call her Mom. And she took the roses I gave you to place them in water, and the whole time she's looking at me with these wide, glowing eyes."

Jordan let out her laughter.

"It's not funny. You didn't tell me how serious your mother was about the whole 'serious beau for you' deal."

"You brought me roses?" Jordan placed her hands on Brian's arms and tried to calm his nerves.

"No. I mean yes. But listen, Jordan, I don't know if I can do this."

"What color are the roses?" Jordan asked, looking up into his beautiful brown eyes. "You know red is my favorite color."

"Jordan!" he whispered. "I'm leaving."

"No, you're not," Jordan said, keeping her eyes focused on his. "We're going to eat a nice turkey dinner and maybe sweet potato pie for dessert, and then my mom will want to talk with you about everything in life for a few hours. Then you can go home, and next week you'll be back in California finishing up your degree, and I will be on the first flight out to Aruba."

"It's going to be okay?" Brian asked. "We're not getting married?"

A sad look entered Jordan's expressive hazel-colored eyes.

"We're not getting married," she affirmed. "But we do need to go to dinner before my parents start worrying about what happened to us."

"Okay," Brian said.

"Okay," Jordan smiled, before giving Brian a kiss.

"We can do this," she said as she took his hands and led him into the dining room.

"Oh, look honey!" Rebecca told her husband of forty years. "They're holding hands."

Brian's knees began to buckle, but Jordan's calm hand on the center of his back helped him stay calm. "Mom," Jordan laughed. "Stop. You're making Brian nervous."

"Well, he may as well get used to us," Rebecca said. "After all, you two are going to get married, right?"

Jordan patted Brian's back which was now trembling.

"Let's eat dinner," Jordan suggested. "And Brian and I can tell you all about the story of us after dessert."

"The story of us?" he whispered. "What are you getting me into?"

"Relax," Jordan whispered back. "This will be over before you know it."

Jordan and Brian settled into chairs next to each other and grew quiet as Jordan's dad prayed over the meal. Brian tried listening to the prayer, but the entire time, he was saying a prayer of his own. *Dear Lord, I love Jordan, but all this marriage talk—even if it just is a charade—is making me nervous. Please get us through this, please!*

~ * ~

"See," Jordan said as she and Brian de-stressed over a tall glass of eggnog. "That wasn't so bad, was it?"

"Jordan," Brian began.

"Yes?"

"What are you going to tell your mom when I return to Cali?"

Jordan waved her hand. "I'll just let her think we're having a long engagement since she already thinks you've proposed, even though I'm not wearing a diamond ring."

"Jordan," Brian said again.

"Yes?" Jordan, who was becoming a bit annoyed, answered.

"We can't keep up this charade. It's wrong."

"I told you. I've got this. Relax."

"Jordan."

"What?" Jordan snapped.

"I won't keep up this charade. You mother loves you, and now she loves me. She's already planning the names of her future grandchildren. I can see it in her eyes."

"What did you expect? You know how my mother is about me getting married."

"Either you tell her the truth," Brian said slowly, "or I'll tell her."

"Fine!" Jordan snapped again, this time with more force as she stood. "Go ahead! Tell my mom that you don't really love me and don't plan to ever marry me, the infamous bachelorette!"

"Jordan." Brian walked to her side and reached for her.

"Leave me alone!"

Gently he took her into his arms and turned her face to his.

"I do love you," he said softly. "I just can't live a lie."

*He loves me?* Jordan thought. The harsh glare in her eyes began to soften. *I love him too.*

"Brian, I'm sorry," Jordan said as her eyes welled up with tears. "I just don't know what else to do."

"You can start by telling your mother how you really feel about the pressure to marry. And you can tell her that I love you dearly, but I'm not ready to marry you yet."

Jordan's eyes grew wide. *He's not ready to marry me yet? Is he saying—no, is he?* "What *are* you saying?"

Brian smiled. "I'm saying that I hope you'll be my girlfriend. This time, though, I'm playing for keeps."

A smile came into full bloom across Jordan's face. "I like the sound of that."

The new couple shared a kiss.

"Now let's go back inside the house," Brian said. "It's getting cold out here on the porch."

The new couple walked inside and took seats by the fireplace, next to Jordan's parents. Rebecca smiled. "We thought you'd be coming in soon," she said. "It is wintertime out there, you know."

"We know, Mom," Jordan replied. "Brian, could you and Dad

get more firewood and help yourself to hot chocolate in the kitchen when you return? Mom and I would like to talk."

"We would?" Rebecca said.

"Yes, Mom. We need to talk."

Mr. Mayfield stood. "Come on, Brian. Let's give the girls some time alone."

While Jordan's dad and her boyfriend bundled up in winter coats and headed outside to gather more firewood, Jordan prayed for strength to say the right thing to her mother and prayed that her mother would not only hear her out, but understand her concerns.

"Mom," Jordan began, "You know I love you, right?"

"Yes, and I love you too sweetie. Now what's wrong?"

"Nothing's wrong. I'd just like to talk with you about the marriage thing."

"Are you worried about planning your wedding? I know this great wedding planner who will work out all the details. She's one of my old friends from college."

Jordan sighed. "See this is exactly what I wanted to talk to you about."

Rebecca's eyes grew wide. "What?"

"With all due respect, Mom, you have been trying to plan my life for me ever since I was born! I need room to breathe, room to think for myself. I need the freedom to make my own decisions and mistakes and to learn from those lessons without you trying to shelter me from all hurt, harm, and danger."

"Well, I'm sorry for being a good mom," Rebecca shot back.

Jordan's eyes grew teary. "You are a good mom. But I'm grown up now. I need my space."

"Move out then, get your own place, and don't visit!"

"Mom," Jordan pleaded as Rebecca stood up and headed for her master bedroom. "That's not what I meant!"

Her only answer was a door slamming.

Jordan sat down and began to cry.

Minutes later, Jordan's dad and boyfriend returned to the family room. "What happened?" her dad asked as Brian went to her side to console her.

"It's pointless." Jordan wiped tears from her eyes. "She doesn't want to listen to me, and now she wants me to leave."

"Don't go anywhere," Jordan's dad said. "Where's your mom?"

"In her bedroom."

"I'll talk to your mother. And you stay with Jordan, Brian."

"Yes, sir," Brian replied.

# The Best Gift

## Chapter 10

Christina smiled then sighed.

"Sounds like somebody's in love."

Christina looked up to see Jesse Villa, one of her fellow photojournalists.

"Yeah," Christina admitted as a silly grin graced her face. "I think I am in love."

"Will this special someone who makes you grin so much be your date to your sister's wedding this weekend?"

"My sister's wedding!" Christina glanced at her watch. "Oh, no!"

Jesse looked at Christina with wide eyes. "What's wrong?"

"Juliette's rehearsal dinner begins in one hour. I forgot I was supposed to leave work early today."

"Hmm, let me take a wild guess at the reason for your sudden memory loss," Jesse said. "Is it because you've had other priorities?"

"Just check the layout of the Roberts' wedding for me," Christina said as she gathered her purse and car keys. "And make any final edits to the page design, would you?"

Jesse shook his head but obliged as he sat at Christina's desk and turned his attention to the page layout on her computer screen.

"Thanks a million," Christina said before running for the elevator.

"Look who's late to her own sister's rehearsal dinner," a dry voice said.

"I'm so sorry." Christina sat next to Juliette before handing her a bag. "But I brought you a gift."

"You're forgiven," Juliette responded as she swiftly accepted the gift. "Besides, you had to leave work early for my event."

"That's right."

"Oh, wow!" Juliette said as she retrieved a beautiful gift card from a women's apparel store. She gave Christina a bear hug. "I love you, sis."

Christina returned the hug. "I love you too."

"Aw," the bridesmaids said as they observed the display of love between two sisters.

"Now, ladies." Juliette returned her attention to her friends. "Let's get this party started!"

Christina turned on the music, and the rehearsal for the wedding began.

But in the back of Christina's mind was a major concern. *I sure hope my dress fits. If not, I'm blaming Eric.*

Ever since Christina agreed to the lunch date with Eric, they'd been spending lunchtime together on a daily basis. Since Christina was tired after a day at work, she'd skipped going to the gym in the morning so she could sleep for two extra hours and still be on time for work.

*With only one day until the wedding, what will I do if the dress doesn't fit?*

~ ✳ ~

Christina stared at herself in the mirror.

*The moment of truth,* she thought as she squeezed into a Spanx full slip which she bought late Saturday night in hopes of making her figure slimmer. A determined yet nervous Christina opened the door to her closet, walked in, and emerged with the maid of honor dress in her hands.

Christina unzipped the beautiful gown and began her familiar shimmy into its fabric.

To her surprise, it fit!

*Praise God!* Having a personal trainer who pushed her to work hard had truly helped her slim down.

*Eating lunch in fancy cafés with Eric didn't help,* Christina thought as she zipped the dress up and realized that her arms were jiggling just a bit. *But it was worth it.*

"Christina!" a boyish voice called from outside her bedroom.

"Yes, Mark?"

"Mom said hurry up. We're waiting on you, and Juliette's getting nervous."

"Tell Mom that I'll be there in a minute. And tell Juliette that it's normal to be nervous on the biggest day of her life."

Christina chuckled as she heard the sound of her brother's running feet.

"He's so cute," Christina said aloud then was hit by another epiphany. *Eric! I didn't tell Eric that the wedding is today!*

"Christina Justine Caballero! Get down here now! Juliette's wedding is in two hours, and it takes one hour to reach the church!"

"I'm leaving now, Mom," Christina called as she grabbed her phone, purse, and keys and hurried out of her room.

"Sorry," she said as she rushed into the white limousine where her entire family was waiting.

"Finally," Juliette said. "Driver, take us to the church!"

⁓ ＊ ⁓

Christina's eyes were tearing up as she watched her baby sister and Matt recite their vows. *I wish I could take pictures from this viewpoint,* she thought.

Flash! Flash!

Christina's eyes followed the blinding light of a professional. Her eyes lit up in pure delight as she saw the person behind the camera—Eric. *What is he doing here?* A blush graced her face as he gave her his famous dazzling smile.

"I now pronounce you husband and wife," the minister declared.

Christina's attention returned to her sister and her new husband just as the minister said, "Matt, you may kiss your bride."

The audience cheered as Matt gently dipped Juliette, tango-style, and planted a kiss on her glossy lips.

"Ladies and gentlemen," the minister said, "I now introduce to you, Mr. and Mrs. Matt Fountaine!"

The newlyweds received cheers and applause. The music played as the couple and the bridal party made their way off the stage and toward the reception hall located next door.

"Christina!"

The familiar voice warmed her heart. She slowed her steps to speak with Eric.

"You look beautiful," he told her.

"Thank you," Christina said. "Who told you that the wedding was today? I'm sorry I forgot to inform you of the time."

"I have my connections," Eric said with a mysterious smile, thinking of his position as the second shooter for the wedding photographer.

"Eric!" Christina's dad called as he approached.

"Dad? How do you know Eric?"

"This fine young man?" Mr. Caballero said. "Why his father and I went to law school together."

"Really? Eric never told me," Christina said.

"You didn't ask," Eric replied with a smile.

"You're staying for dinner, right, son?"

"Yes, sir."

"Good. We've set an extra space for you at our family's table."

*My dad saved a seat for Eric at the family table?* Christina thought. *Wow, he must know Eric and his father real well.*

"Thank you, sir," Eric said.

"And you take good care of my daughter," Mr. Caballero said.

"Dad!"

"I will, sir," Eric assured Christina's dad. "She's the best."

"Yes," Mr. Caballero said as he held the door open for the wedding party and guests. "She and her sister take after their mother."

"Thanks, Dad," Christina said as she walked through the door.

"Can we talk over coffee tomorrow?" Eric asked.

"Sure," Christina replied. "Meet me at the café?"

"See you there," Eric replied, agreeing to meet at their favorite lunch date place as he escorted Christina to the reception hall.

"Wow, he's hot, and he's famous," Bessie, one of the bridesmaids, remarked.

"You know him?" Christina asked.

"Duh! Everyone knows Eric Hazelton."

The bridesmaids stood with their appointed groomsmen at their sides, waiting by the entrance to the dining hall to be introduced before the bride and groom.

"Ready to catch the wedding bouquet?" Bessie whispered.

"No, why?"

"It doesn't matter if you do, because I already know that you're next. Have you seen the way Eric looks at you? And the way your dad speaks with him? Girl, you've got family's favor and God's favor because obviously He was the one who orchestrated your meeting Eric, however that happened."

Christina took a walk down memory lane and smiled, realizing that Bessie was right.

*Meeting Eric was part of God's plan for my life. And I'm going to trust God to show me what's next.*

# *The Best Gift*

# Epilogue

*J*ordan stood in line at the airport, ready to register her plane ticket to Aruba. A wintery mix of snow and sleet had delayed her flight, but in an airport bookstore, she'd found a book on God's promises for women and read through it while she waited.

*For I know the plans I have for you, thus saith the Lord, plans to prosper you and not to harm you, plans to give you hope and a future.*

"Interesting," Jordan said aloud before turning her attention to the shuffling she heard in the long line.

"Excuse me," a voice insisted as someone pushed through the crowd. "Excuse me!"

Jordan had sneaked out of the house early Monday morning and left a note for her family that she was on her way to Aruba. So she wasn't expecting anybody she knew to be at the airport. But there were her parents and Brian, pushing their way through the crowd to get to her place in line.

"Your mother has something tell you," Mr. Mayfield said. "Then Brian and I will return."

Brian and Jordan's dad walked a little distance away while Jordan's mother approached.

"I'm sorry," she said simply. "I've had time to think about what you said, and when I read the note you left for your father and me—" Mrs. Mayfield began to cry. "I just realized that my baby girl is all grown-up and has been for several years. And I realized how wrong it is of me to place so much pressure on you to get married sooner than later. Will you forgive me?"

Jordan's eyes grew teary. "I forgive you, Mom," she said as she gave her a hug. "Now that we've forgiven each other, want to hear a funny story?"

"Sure," Rebecca said as she wiped her eyes.

"It all started when Brian returned home for the holidays." Jordan told her mother the truth about how a charade she agreed to with Brian turned into something serious.

Minutes later, her mother looked at Jordan in surprise.

"So you and Brian are officially together now?"

Jordan nodded and waved at Brian who stood in the distance. "Since Christmas Day."

"I'm happy for you," she said. "But I will not rush you two to get married."

Jordan laughed. "Thanks, Mom."

"Everything okay, ladies?" Mr. Mayfield asked as he and Brian approached with caution.

"Yes," Jordan and her mother replied in unison.

"Flight 472 has been delayed until further notice, due to inclement weather." The announcement reverberated throughout the waiting area. "Please make other plans for tonight."

"I say we all go home," Mr. Mayfield said before looking at his daughter. "You don't really want to spend New Year's in Aruba without your family and Brian, do you?"

"No," Jordan admitted. "It wouldn't be the same without you all."

"I say we brave the weather and go home."

"I second that motion," Brian agreed.

"All in favor say aye," Mr. Mayfield said.

"Aye!" everyone said in unison.

Jordan smiled as she closed her gift book and Brian helped her with her luggage.

*God's Word is true,* she thought referring to the Bible text she'd read. *He only has great plans for our lives.*

~ * ~

Christina smiled at Eric over her glass of green tea. It was the Monday after her sister's wedding, and they were meeting for what was now their regular scheduled lunch at Carina's Café, an upscale restaurant where they'd met for their first lunch date two weeks ago.

"Hi," a familiar voice greeted. "You two look familiar."

Christina and Eric stopped staring into each other's eyes long enough to look up at the source of the voice—Carina, their waitress from their first date.

"Hi," Eric said. "You look familiar too."

Carina let out a rich peal of laughter. "Oh, that's right. You're the lovely couple I thought were married."

"I'm Carina Carter," the young girl said. "My husband owns this café, and I help run it."

"Really?" Christina said. "But you look so young."

Carina laughed again before replying, "Having five children and chasing after them keeps you young."

"Five children?" Christina said, sharing a look with an equally surprised Eric. *She's so thin.*

Carina nodded her head in affirmation. "Five—each one year apart."

"Wow."

"Yeah, we love our little munchkins. Now what can I get you two?"

"Sparkling water with lemon," they answered in unison.

Carina's eyes sparkled. "Now why does that line sound familiar?"

Christina blushed and Eric grinned.

"You know," Carina said as she returned with their sparkling water with lemon, "our restaurant caters weddings. And our favorite frequent customers get a discount on the final price, as a wedding gift from our hearts to yours."

Eric flashed his dazzling smile at Christina, causing her heart to melt.

"Think about it," Carina suggested before whipping out her notepad and a pen. "May I take your order?"

"One mega spaghetti bowl," Eric said, holding Christina's gaze with his piercing brown eyes.

"Feta cheese on a garden salad," Christina said, somehow managing not to waver beneath Eric's gaze.

"And some privacy?" Carina guessed.

When Eric and Christina didn't answer, Carina nodded. "I'll be right back with your order."

"Christina," Eric began.

"Yes?"

"What are you doing for the rest of your life?"

A smile tugged at the corner of her lips. "Why?"

"I'd like to know."

"Why?"

"Because I'd like to spend the rest of my life with you."

"Why?"

"Because."

"Because?"

"I—" He took Christina's hands in his. "Love—" He leaned forward, and Christina met him halfway. "You," he whispered.

The couple shared a kiss and realized that it marked the beginning of a beautiful love story—their own.

~ * ~

Joshua walked into Stonehenge Church with Julie and her sister Reba by his side. Reba, who was nervous, shook as she stood in the lobby.

"Relax, sis," Julie said as she placed a hand on her sister's back. "You're going to be happy you visited today."

"The young adult group meets upstairs," Joshua said as he began to lead his company toward the stairwell.

Reba paused. "I don't know if I can do this."

After much prayer in the hospital and at the Stonehenge Church for Reba, she found herself recovering from her nervous breakdown. She was released from the hospital two days ago and advised to take it easy, along with a daily dose of medicine for her nerves.

"You can do this, Re," Julie said calmly to her sister. "The church is like a hospital for humanity. You're in the right place."

"Expect healing," Joshua added. "It may not come immediately, but when you stand on holy ground, every prayer is heard and God will answer you before you speak."

"Before I speak?"

"Yes," Julie and Joshua said in unison.

"Okay," Reba said. "Let's go."

Minutes later, Joshua and his company entered the Sabbath School classroom.

"Morning, Josh," Mariska was leading worship that morning. "We were just about to sing our praise songs before lesson study. Welcome."

"Good morning, Mari," Joshua returned before gesturing to his friends. "Class, these are my friends—Julie and her sister Reba."

"Morning, Julie and Reba!" the crowd of twenty young adults greeted enthusiastically, causing a smile to tug at Reba's lips.

"Good morning," Julie returned.

Reba timidly nodded.

"Let's have a seat," Joshua whispered to his company.

Mariska turned on the sound system, and a beautiful song began to play. "We're going to sing some worship songs and then we'll get into the lesson for today."

It took only a moment for everyone to stand and the beautiful music to fill the room.

As Reba listened to the song, silent tears began to roll down her cheeks. She felt Joshua and her sister wrap an arm around her waist. Reba wiped tears from her eyes and felt grateful for being in good company and for their support. Minutes later, Mariska asked everyone to bow their heads for prayer.

"Dear God," Mariska prayed as the music faded into the background and everyone became silent. "We need you now. Please reign in our lives, live in our hearts, and shine through our eyes and the way we live so that others may come to know You and love you and live for You. Please help us to be ready when You return to take us home. In Jesus' name we pray, Amen."

As Reba opened her eyes and took a seat with the rest of the class, she felt different. It was as if God was working on her heart and speaking to her spirit, and somehow she knew that, though it may not be easy, everything would be okay.

"Are you okay?" Julie whispered as they sat.

"Yes," Reba replied slowly. "I am okay."

Joshua and Julie each took one of Reba's hands in theirs. The company of three joined the company of believers and engaged in a discussion over the lesson study.

A feeling of peace settled over the believers in the room, and a feeling of conviction settled into Joshua's spirit. *Thank You, Jesus,* he prayed, *for blessing me and keeping us all in Your care. Please continue to reveal Your plan, Your will, Your purpose for all our lives. We love You, Lord. In Your Name I pray, Amen.*

"It's going to be a beautiful New Year," Julie whispered to Joshua.

Joshua nodded. *Life is beautiful,* he thought. *And worth living when you know God is in control.*

# Book Three:

## *Peace and Love*

*Peace and Love*

# Chapter 1

*E*lle Brighton drove her black BMW coupe into the guest parking lot of the Four Seasons Hotel. "Look, baby," she said, talking to her car, "there's your cousin, the BMW convertible. I think you're a lot cuter, but we're going to park next to your kin, okay?"

Elle laughed at her own attempt at humor. Talking to herself—and her BMW—was one of her quirks. People either thought she was crazy or gifted as an actress. Elle, who lived off of freelance work as an artist, believed that to be successful in the world of arts, a person had to be a combination of both crazy and gifted.

Elle exited her car and locked the doors. She then opened the trunk and tugged out her oversized purple Traveler's suitcase. Elle turned her eyes heavenward and sent up a silent prayer for success in her job hunt.

*The holiday season is going to be beautiful,* she thought. *I just know it.*

~ * ~

Kristine Amanda Thompson paused in the photo frame aisle at Target. Her gaze fixed on a beautiful silver frame with the words *Mother and Daughter* engraved across the bottom. Tears welled up in her eyes as she picked up the lovely design.

*Maybe this year will be different,* she thought, gently placing the frame into the shopping cart.

Kristine worked as a senior sales associate at Stylish Comfort—an upscale women's apparel store in downtown Atlanta, Georgia. With her reliability, natural kindness, and demand for excellence, everyone—including Kristine—believed she'd be first choice for the manager position this holiday season. But the promotion was the furthest thing on Kristine's wish list. She only wanted one thing—to be reunited with her birth mom.

After graduating from college and moving back into her adoptive parents' house, she told them what she'd been thinking for years—she wanted to know who her birth mother was. Now, as an adult engaged to marry her college sweetheart on Valentine's Day, Kristine very much wanted to find her birth mother. It was tough for her to do all the planning for the wedding with her adoptive parents and fiancé Derek, but not with the woman who gave her life.

Kristine picked up the empty picture frame and gazed at it once more. *Please, Lord, if it is Your will, bless my search for my birth mother. You've blessed me with adoptive parents who love me, and I am forever grateful. But You understand that there's a hole in my heart that can only be filled with the love of my birth mom. Please, Lord, help me find her. In Jesus' name I pray, Amen.*

⁓ ✱ ⁓

Eric Stewart sighed out of exasperation. Not again. Not this Christmas.

He was looking at the brief for his latest family law case—what looked like a very nasty divorce. While Eric enjoyed his job, there was a bit of irony to it. There was Eric, a family law attorney who prosecuted everything from divorce cases to custody battles, yet he couldn't get his own life straight in the category of romance.

He blamed it all on his parents who suffered a bitter divorce when he was only fifteen. Life had not been the same since. Despite being a twenty-eight-year-old man, Eric still harbored resentment over his parents' failed marriage. Now, years later, Eric was more resentful than ever, and the holiday season just made him more of a Scrooge.

"Why did you have to do it?" Eric, who rarely talked to himself, said aloud.

"Why did who have to do what?" a feminine voice inquired.

Eric turned his attention from his memories to his paralegal Rebecca Heart. "It's nothing, Rebecca. How may I help you?"

"Are you okay?" she asked. "Should I get you a latte?"

*All the lattes in the world aren't going to help me.* He smiled at Rebecca's thoughtfulness. "That's very sweet of you, but no, I don't need coffee."

Rebecca smiled. "Okay. Well, have a happy holiday season."

Eric managed a small smile. "Thanks Rebecca." He turned his attention to the case briefing on his desk. "Hey, have you talked to Bridget Andersen?"

"Yes, she calls every day asking for you."

"Thank you for not telling me."

Rebecca tried not to show frustration. "But you told me that you always call your clients first."

"Rebecca, it's okay," Eric said. "I have to phone both parties tomorrow morning. If Mrs. Andersen calls before then, let her know I will be in touch with her soon."

"Okay. Have a good night," Rebecca said before leaving for her desk.

Eric looked at his wall clock. Seven o'clock. *Wasn't there something I had to do at seven?*

"Rebecca!" Eric called.

She rushed into the inner office with her agenda book in hand.

"Don't I have something planned for tonight? Check the calendar."

She quickly flipped through the book to December first. Her face fell.

"What's wrong?"

"Nothing," she said, looking up at him and trying to hide her disappointment. "You have a date with Mariana Santiago tonight, and you're supposed to pick her up right now."

Eric began to pack his briefcase and grabbed his coat. He handed his office keys to her. "Lock up the office when you leave, would you?"

Rebecca nodded.

"And don't stay here too late."

Rebecca nodded again.

As Eric rushed out of the door for the elevator, his Blackberry to his ear, Rebecca locked the door and settled into her chair. She took a look at the clock and then at the remaining stack of work due tomorrow morning.

*Another late night,* she thought, *spent working.*

Quietly, Rebecca began to type.

# Chapter 2

Beautiful, radiant rays of sunlight streamed through the vertical blinds which covered the balcony doors in Elle's second floor room at the Four Seasons Hotel. A yawn escaped as she stretched and opened her eyes which trailed to the alarm clock on the night stand. "Great, I've got two hours before my interview," Elle realized as she rolled out of bed and onto her knees to say her prayers before taking a shower.

Part of the reason Elle was in Maryland was because her job search had landed her four interviews—two in Virginia, one in Maryland, and one in Washington, D.C. The final interview was to take place at a prestigious art company in Washington, D.C., on December twenty which was only three days before she traveled to Westminster, Virginia, to spend the final week of the holidays with her cousins.

It was tradition for Elle and her cousins to meet at their Auntie Charlotte's sprawling mansion. The beauty of it all was that they always met someone new—Charlotte's mansion was used during the holidays as a bed and breakfast for out-of-towners.

After showering and dressing to the nines in a two-piece emerald-green blazer and black pumps, Elle applied lip gloss, mascara, eye shadow, and a bit of blush to her cheeks. She pulled her hair back into a tight ponytail, filed her fingernails, and glossed them with rose-petal pink polish.

Elle checked her final look in the mirror, smiled, grabbed her purse, donned her black winter coat, and walked to the elevator which took her to the main lobby. As Elle walked through the lobby with the full intention of going straight to her car, the sweet aroma of the hotel's complimentary breakfast captivated her.

*I need to eat a good breakfast,* Elle rationalized, *and it shouldn't take me too long to get to Baltimore.*

Deciding that it would be unhealthy not to eat breakfast, Elle made a detour to the breakfast café.

~ * ~

Songs of the Christmas season drifted sweetly from the underground speakers at the outdoor mall where Kristine worked.

But today she was oblivious because she was running late to work—literally—in three-inch heels. Kristine glanced at her wristwatch as she approached the doors to the building.

"Five minutes," she said, noting the amount of time for which she was late and trying not to fret.

Kristine had a reputation for being on time or early each and every day. Surely missing five minutes wouldn't be too detrimental to her career. Quickly, she found her way to the employee's lounge where she placed her purse and coat into her locker and smoothed the slight wrinkles in her forest green pencil skirt and white button-down blouse. Satisfied with her appearance, Kristine walked briskly to her station in the coat and evening wear gallery.

Kristine froze as she stood two feet from the station where Lila Bleu, her boss and the store's general manager, was finishing a transaction with a customer.

"Thank you for shopping at Stylish Comfort," Lila told the customer as she handed the shopping bag to the patron. "And Happy Holidays."

The customer smiled, took her shopping bag, and left.

"Good morning, Kristine," Lila greeted her most reliable employee with a dry smile.

"Please accept my apologies, Lila. I had an appointment before work, and that's why I'm five minutes late."

"Ten," Lila said. "You are ten minutes late to work."

Kristine looked puzzled before she realized that she must have spent five additional minutes in the employee lounge. "I'm sorry," she apologized once more. "It will not happen again."

"Given how busy we are over the holiday season, it better not happen again."

"Yes, ma'am, it won't."

"Good," said Lila. "I have a meeting to attend. Good day."

As Lila left the gallery, Kristine assumed her position behind the cash register and silently chastised herself for being late.

*I hope that Paulo knows what he's doing.*

The reason she was late was because she had an appointment with Paulo Riviera, the private investigator she'd hired to find her birth mom. Paulo had called Kristine to tell her that he had a lead in northern Maryland. There was a good chance that he'd found someone who knew her mother and if he was correct, her mother lived somewhere in Maryland. Paulo needed to know if Kristine was willing to spend a few days before Christmas in Maryland. Kristine agreed. He told her to book a hotel and buy a Christmas present because he had a good feeling about this lead.

*If Paulo's on to something and this lead helps me to find my birth mom, I'll be able to celebrate Christmas with the one person I've been hoping to meet all my life.*

~ \* ~

"I've been trying to reach you all week," the angry caller berated her attorney. "I don't pay you to play phone tag."

Eric placed his head in his free hand. "I'm sorry, Mrs. Andersen—"

"Don't call me that!"

Eric sighed. "What should I call you, ma'am?"

"Bridget. Call me Bridget. I can't stand to be called anything that reminds me of *him*."

"So, Bridget, when would you like to meet to discuss your case?"

"As soon as possible."

"That can be arranged. May I place you on hold? I need to consult my paralegal."

"You have one minute," Bridget said.

Eric touched the *hold* button then pressed the extension for Rebecca's office phone.

"Good morning, Eric," Rebecca chirped. "How may I help you?"

"I have Bridget on hold. She'd like to schedule a consultation ASAP. What's my schedule look like?"

"Let me see," Rebecca said as she pulled out the agenda book which contained Eric's schedule for the next five months.

"You have an hour opening today at five o'clock in the evening."

"Pencil Mrs. Andersen in for that slot. And be sure to only address her as Bridget if she calls again."

"Yes, sir," Rebecca replied as she opened the scheduling database and finalized the appointment. "She's booked. You just need to confirm the time with Bridget."

"Thanks, Rebecca. You're the best."

Rebecca felt a blush creep onto her face and was immediately grateful that he could not see her.

"Two minutes," Bridget said as soon as Eric picked up the phone line.

"I'm sorry?"

"Sorry doesn't cut it, mister. You had me wait one extra minute."

"As opposed to?"

"As opposed to the one minute I gave you. Listen, *Eric*, I may be getting a divorce, but I am extremely well-off financially and I can hire a new attorney for my case at any minute. But I won't because I think you're one of the best defending attorneys Manhattan has to offer, and you better hear me when I say that I want to win my case!"

*I hear you loud and clear—very loud and very clear,* Eric thought. "I understand your passion for settling this case. This is why we'd like for you to visit our office today at five o'clock. I need to know all the details before I can proceed."

"I'll be there," Bridget confirmed.

"It's settled then. See you at five." He hung up the telephone and rubbed his ears which literally hurt after being shouted at.

*Divorce cases,* he thought. *It's a battle nobody ever truly wins.*

# Peace and Love

# Chapter 3

Elle stared at the art canvas before her. She had botched her first interview—and it was all because she'd tried to have a healthy start to her morning. After eating breakfast, Elle had taken to the Beltway, only to find herself in rush-hour traffic. Needless to say, she hadn't arrived for her interview until one hour after her scheduled appointment.

The receptionist took one look at Elle's interview time in her scheduler and frowned. "I'm sorry, miss," the lady told her, "but you're an hour late and Mr. Stillwater does not accept tardiness."

"What are you saying?"

"I'm saying that your interview has been terminated."

"May I reschedule?"

"I'm sorry, but Mr. Stillwater does not make exceptions for anyone."

"But I brought all my best work!" Elle protested as she laid out three canvases and a portfolio case upon the front desk.

"You have to leave now, or I will call security."

Her heart dropped, but she obeyed the receptionist's orders and left the building.

Now Elle sat staring at a blank canvas, thinking of its parallels to her life.

*One day,* Elle thought, *I'll have my own art gallery and help other starving artists get their work recognized, bought, and sold. One day I'll help others who are feeling like their lives are a blank canvas. I just have to help myself first.*

Elle then thought of the only One who could take her where she needed to go, the only One whose timing was perfect. Elle took out her Bible and began to read the wisdom in the book of Proverbs 3:5-6.

"Trust in the Lord with all your heart," she recited aloud, reading from the New International Version, "And lean not on your own understanding; in all your ways submit to him, and he will make your paths straight."

*Dear God,* she prayed, *please order my steps and help me to trust completely in Your Word. In Jesus' name I pray, Amen.*

～ ✳ ～

Eric stared at the basket case before him, who was going through her second box of tissues as she cried what would soon be a river. *This is not the same lady who yelled at me over the telephone.*

"Bridget," Eric said, taking a seat next to her on his office couch, "you'll be okay."

Bridget had walked into his office on time, looking cool and composed, but once he asked her to tell him the story of why she wanted a divorce, she burst into tears. Fifteen minutes later, the waterworks were still flowing.

"No, I—" She sobbed between each word. "I won't—be okay."

Eric sighed. Maybe Rebecca could console her, because at this rate, they were never going to get any work done.

Eric walked to his desk and paged Rebecca.

"Yes, Eric?"

"I need you in here."

"Yes, sir."

Rebecca stopped what she was working on and walked into

Eric's office to see the reason why he needed her help. *The sobbing female client,* she thought. *This is only the tip of the iceberg.*

"Bridget," Rebecca said, taking a seat next to the inconsolable woman. "I know you won't believe me at this moment, but everything really will be okay. Eric's an excellent attorney. You couldn't have anyone better working for you." Rebecca leaned in for the tried-and-true soother. "And did I tell you that he wins *every case?*"

The sobbing stopped. Bridget looked up at Eric then Rebecca. "Really?"

Rebecca nodded.

"Well, then," Bridget said as she wiped the tears from her face. "Where shall we start?"

Eric smiled. "Thank you for your assistance, Rebecca."

She nodded and left.

He took out a legal-sized notepad and pen and sat in a chair across from the couch. "Let's begin," he told Bridget.

"It all started when he began working late at the office every night."

Eric took notes while she talked, hoping that he would be able to go home soon after this meeting.

# *Peace and Love*

# Chapter 4

K ristine held up the green, red, and gold scarf and matching hat for her fiancé Derek Jensen to see. "What do you think?"

When Derek paused with a hand under his chin, Kristine knew he didn't like the gift. "Give me your honest opinion."

"It's—" Derek started, knowing from experience that he needed to choose his words carefully. "Creative."

Kristine nodded and folded the scarf, placing it and the hat back into the gift bag which was decorated with snowflakes.

"Kristine," Derek said, taking his fiancée's slender hands into his work-worn ones. "I know you're excited about meeting your mom, but why don't you wait until you meet her so you know what she likes? It might save your wallet a lot of money if you two just went to lunch and then shopped together."

"But I want her to know that I love her."

Derek smiled. "Kristine, sweetie, I think your birth mother loves you more than you can ever love her."

"Then why did she give me up for adoption?"

"That is something you'll have to ask her when you two are reunited."

His attention caught on the silver picture frame with *Mother and Daughter* engraved across the bottom. "What's this?"

"Something I picked up at the store a little while ago. You like it?"

"Yes. Why don't you give this to your mother?"

"What if she doesn't want to meet me?"

"Okay," Derek sighed. "Who are you and what have you done with the woman I plan to marry?"

Kristine gave Derek a look. "What do you mean?"

"The Kristine Amanda Thompson I know is feisty, brilliant— did I mention beautiful?—*and* she doesn't let any daunting task overwhelm her, whether it's learning to ice-skate or, in this case, meet her mother."

Kristine began to laugh.

"Yeah," Derek said. "You know I'm right."

His words resonated with her. "You're right," she told him. "I'm just nervous. I'll get over it. But ice skating? I've never even walked on ice."

"Oh, I didn't tell you?" Derek inquired.

"Tell me what?"

A grin spread across Derek's face as he reached for the big bag he had carried with him.

"Merry Christmas, baby," he told her as he gave her his traditional pre-Christmas gift.

"Derek, you didn't," Kristine said as she retrieved a beautiful pair of white leather ice skates.

"I did."

"But I don't know *how* to ice skate."

Derek continued to grin.

"No," Kristine said as if reading his thoughts. "Take these back."

"I'm not taking them back. But I am going to teach you how to skate like the stars."

"Dance like the stars, I can do," Kristine said. "But skate like a pro is not something I can achieve—even in my dreams."

"Well." Derek kept his hands in his jean pockets so that he could not take the skates.

"Well?" Kristine countered.

"Think about it."

"I've thought about it, and the answer, Derek, is no."

"Sleep on it. Then meet me at the downtown ice skating rink tomorrow morning."

"Derek, I said no. I am not an ice skater, and I do not ever intend to touch the ice and—."

Kristine paused as she realized that Derek had donned his coat and grabbed his car keys.

"I love you," he said, taking her into his arms and planting a kiss on her forehead. "And I'll see you at the skating rink tomorrow at ten. Don't be late."

Kristine swooned.

"Whew," she said as she locked her front door after Derek had driven away. "Five years, and he *still* makes me swoon."

But learn how to ice skate? That was not happening. Not this Christmas.

Kristine feared falling and breaking a leg, something that would impede her plans to travel to Maryland to visit her mother. *If Derek thinks he's going to get me to wear these skates, much less use them on ice, then he is about to be disappointed. I'm not taking any risks. Not now.*

Kristine took a look at the skates' sleek design. *They are really pretty, though. If only I knew how to skate.* At the thought of reconsidering, Kristine shook her head, placed the bag on the floor, and headed into her kitchen to fix dinner.

~ * ~

Eric rushed into the upscale restaurant and met the receptionist.

"How may I help you, sir?"

"Table for two," Eric said. "Reserved for Santiago."

The receptionist scanned the reservations and seating chart on the computer then looked at Eric. "I'm sorry, sir, but she left an hour ago."

"An hour?" Eric asked, looking at his watch and feeling his heart sink to his stomach. He was supposed to meet Mariana two hours ago.

As he walked to his car, Eric picked up his Blackberry to call Mariana. He noticed there was a message in his voicemail. It was from Mariana. Listening to it might not be a good idea, but he wanted to know what she thought.

"Eric," she began in her strong Peruvian accent, "I cannot even describe in words how mad I am at you right now! When you arrived at my house two hours late for our first date, I forgave you because you were so sweet and promised you'd make it up to me. But here I am, sitting by myself at this beautiful restaurant where you promised to meet me for dinner. And guess what? You're not here!

"Eric, I thought that I liked you and that you deserved a second chance. But now I see that I don't matter to you, either that or you just can't fit me into your busy schedule. Both reasons are enough for me to never want to see you again. Goodbye, Eric. Don't call me because I will not talk to you."

Eric sighed as he slid into the driver's seat of his sports car.

~ * ~

In the hotel gym, Elle worked out on the elliptical, scrolling through the music list on her iPod.

"What songs are you listening to?" someone asked.

Elle glanced sideways at the petite lady. Her gym clothes might be outdated, but she had a friendly smile. "Monica," Elle said. "She has a Christmas album."

"Oh, that's awesome," the lady said before extending her hand. "I'm Mandy Dawson. A pleasure to meet you."

Elle shook her hand. "Elle Brighton."

"Well, it is a pleasure to meet you, Elle. What do you do for a living?"

*I'm a starving artist. Got food?* "I'm a freelancer for print stories, and I paint and sell my canvas artwork as a side business."

Mandy's eyes lit up. "What type of artwork?"

Elle shrugged. Why was this lady asking so many questions? "Oh, you know, stuff."

Mandy smiled, sensing that Elle did not want to talk. An idea struck Mandy, and she dug into her fanny pack and retrieved one of her business cards. "I work for the Art Institute in Arlington, Virginia," she said. "I teach the core fashion courses and am looking for a personal assistant. Look me up and contact me before New Year's Day if you're interested."

Elle accepted the business card. *Fashion. Hm, never gave a thought to that career field.*

Mandy pressed the reset button on her elliptical and took a long sip of water from her water bottle. She hopped off of the machine and waved goodbye.

"Goodbye," Elle said. She kept staring at the business card. *Could this be the job for me?*

The thought was dismissed with a shrug. *I'll call her after my final interview.*

Elle's heart was set on landing the fourth and final interview with the National Endowment for the Arts in Washington, D.C. Elle had done her homework—it would be her dream job.

*Dreams do come true. I just know it.*

*Peace and Love*

# Chapter 5

*I can't believe I'm doing this,* Kristine thought as she approached the recreation center. Against her better judgment, she'd decided to meet Derek at the ice rink for skating lessons.

"Morning, love," Derek, who was waiting by the front doors in the lobby, greeted his fiancée with a kiss.

Kristine sighed. "Derek, you better know how to ice skate. I don't feel like breaking a leg."

Derek laughed and led her by the hand to the Olympic-sized ice rink.

Derek already had his ice skates on his feet. He'd been walking with skate covers so the blades wouldn't scratch the floor. Kristine sat on the bleachers. "I don't know if this is a good idea. It's Sunday, and I've got to go to work tomorrow. I have a feeling I'm going to break something."

"Kristine," Derek said. "Relax. I won't let you fall."

She sighed as she retrieved her ice skates from the bag. "All right."

Five minutes later, Derek led her onto the cold ice.

And the ice skating lessons began.

~ * ~

"Eric?" Rebecca asked timidly as she knocked on her boss's door.

It was five o'clock on Monday morning, and she had come to work early to finish a major project. As she'd placed her purse under lock and key, she realized that she was hearing Christmas music playing somewhere behind Eric's closed door.

"Eric?" she called again, wondering what was going on. Maybe she should call security.

Just as she reached for the phone, the door opened, and Rebecca saw a very sleepy, disheveled Eric.

"Are you okay?" she asked. "What are you doing at work so early?" Eric might stay late, but she'd never seen him at work before seven in the morning.

"I had work to finish," Eric said. "What time is it?"

"Five o'clock in the morning. Were you here all night?"

Eric yawned and rubbed his eyes. "Looks like it."

She peered into his office. It was a disheveled mess. Papers were everywhere. "Maybe you should take the first half of the day off."

"Good idea." He grabbed his wallet and car keys. "I'll see you this afternoon. Would you mind organizing my office? You do such a great job organizing the office space."

Reluctantly she agreed, even though she had other things to do. He left, and Rebecca stared blankly at the mess before her.

"Never let a task look too challenging," she repeated over and over as she began to organize Eric's office.

She deserved a pay raise.

~ \* ~

*Interview number three,* Elle thought as she ate a bagel with cream cheese in the hotel breakfast café, *I'm going to be on time just for you.*

Ten minutes later, Elle was on the road, driving to Annapolis, Maryland, to interview for a job as a page designer with the city newspaper. Elle held a degree in English and a minor in graphic arts which made her a perfect candidate for a wide variety of jobs in the arts. If she could only be on time for her interviews, she might actually have a chance at being hired. One hour on the road passed, and Elle found herself searching for a parking space in the lot opposite the *Annapolis Times*.

As Elle pulled into what she believed was the last empty parking space, she glanced at her car's digital clock. "Nine a.m., and I've got ten minutes to spare," she announced proudly as she turned off the ignition, grabbed her purse, and shut the car door.

After a couple minutes of waiting in the lobby, a tall, willowy woman met Elle. "Good morning, I'm Pearl Towson, Mr. Crest's personal assistant," she said. "Follow me. Mr. Crest is expecting you."

Pearl led Elle to the fifth floor where a sharply dressed business man sat behind a desk in a lavishly decorated office. "Good day Ms. Brighton," he greeted as he stood and they shook hands.

"Good day, Mr. Crest," Elle said. "It's a pleasure to meet you."

"Have a seat, please." He waited until she sat. "Tell me about yourself."

"I am an artist and writer. I've sold several paintings, and a good amount of my articles have been published. I hold a degree in English and a minor in Graphic Design. I'm quite flexible, and I strive to always meet my deadlines."

Mr. Crest nodded. "Now why would you like the job as a page-design editor?"

"I'm very artistic and technical in my approach to design. I know the rules, and I won't break them unless told to do so. My work is well presented, and I'm not afraid to edit. That's why I think I'd be a great candidate for this job."

Twenty minutes later, Elle left the building with high hopes that she'd finally landed a stable job for the New Year.

*Peace and Love*

# Chapter 6

Kristine sat in the Emergency Room in the city hospital with Derek beside her. She'd fallen on the ice and twisted her right ankle.

"I told you trying to teach me how to skate was a bad idea. I bet I broke my ankle."

Derek knew what a broken bone looked like, and this wasn't it. "Kristine, if it had been broken, you'd be screaming in pain right now."

"Whatever!" she snapped. "Next time I'm going with my gut."

"Admit it."

"Admit what?"

"You had fun—right until you twisted your ankle. And that's all it is. It will heal before December twentieth, I promise."

"December twentieth?" Kristine voiced aloud. "Oh no, December twentieth!"

"What's wrong?"

"I'm supposed to drive up to Maryland!"

"Relax. If your ankle doesn't heal by then, I'll drive you."

"Really?" She faced him. "You can take two weeks off work, just like that?"

Derek laughed.

"What?"

*She's so cute when she's angry and trying to act tough.* "Kristine, you'll get through this. I wanted to go with you so I've taken leave from December twentieth until January second."

"Aw, you're so wonderful!" She gave him a hug. "Except when you let me fall."

"If I recall correctly, I picked you up off the ice and carried you to the car, then drove you to the ER."

"What's your point?"

"That I love you and I'm here for you."

"I love you too, Derek. But don't you think it will be a bit too much for both of us to meet my mom?"

"I'm going to be visiting my sister while you take care of business."

Derek's sister lived in northern Maryland where she worked as a teacher. She would be on Christmas break, and Derek thought it was the perfect opportunity to visit his family.

"Kristine Thompson?"

Derek and Kristine looked up to see a lady dressed in slacks, a black top, and a white doctor's work coat. She stood by the door leading to the treatment center, waiting.

"Come on," Derek said, standing up and holding out his hand.

Kristine took his hand then swung her arm over his shoulder, leaning on him like a human crutch as together they made their way to the doctor.

~ * ~

Eric sat behind his office desk, patiently drafting his argument for Bridget's case.

There was knocking at his door.

"Come in," Eric said.

Rebecca walked into the office, looking very much under the weather.

"What's wrong?" he asked.

"I don't feel well," Rebecca said. "May I leave for the day? I'd like to make an appointment with the doctor."

"Yes, please go," Eric said. "Your health is important."

"Thanks, Eric."

"No problem."

Rebecca gathered her purse and notebook and left the building.

Eric looked over his notes. According to Bridget, Mr. Andersen was an alcoholic, and when he was under the influence, he would insult Bridget, smash plates, and throw books and other lightweight objects across whichever room he was in.

While Eric was saddened by this, what made him even sadder was the fact that the Andersen couple had a fifteen-year-old daughter who often witnessed his intoxicated behavior.

The case brought back memories of Eric's childhood. His father and mother divorced when he was fifteen because of the way Eric's dad behaved when he, too, was under the influence of alcohol. Eric's mother flew to Tahiti out of anger, fell in love with the island, and decided to move there. It was the last he'd ever heard of his mother.

Since his mother abandoned Eric, his dad won custody on one condition—that Eric's dad check into rehab and quit his alcoholic ways. Eric was surprised that his dad, who had a tendency to be stubborn, actually did check into rehab and emerged victorious. Eric lived with him until he started college. But still he would not forgive his parents for divorcing—or his mother for abandoning him.

Eric placed his head in his hands. *It is the holiday season. Maybe I should go visit Dad.*

Eric gave up on ever seeing his mother again, but his dad still lived in Seattle, an entire continent away from New York.

*I should call first.*

They hadn't spoken since he'd moved out of the house. Eric picked up his phone and dialed his familiar old number.

The phone rang twice then the answering machine sounded.

"Hi, Dad. It's me—Eric. I was just thinking about you and decided to call you. Why don't you call me back when you have time?"

Eric gave his dad his number and hung up.

~ * ~

Elle sighed. *When am I going to finally land a job?*

She'd heard from her first two interviewers today—neither employer wanted to hire her and to make matters worse, Elle also received an e-mail from her third interviewer, saying that they'd decided to hire another candidate who was better qualified for the job.

*One more interview.* She thought of her final interview tomorrow at the art gallery in Washington, D.C. *One last chance.*

*Peace and Love*

# Chapter 7

*I*f she hadn't been seated in a chair, Kristine would have fallen to the floor.

She'd been ambling around her apartment on crutches, trying to dust, when the phone rang. Paulo was on the line with good news—he had found her birth mother. It was news Kristine had waited her whole life to hear, but she'd never imagined the discovery would render her speechless.

"Kristine, are you still there?"

She nodded her head before realizing Paulo could not see her. "Yes, Paulo. I'm here."

"Your birth mother's name is Colleen Roma," he said. "She is forty-years-old, widowed, and lives in a single family home in the suburbs of northern Maryland."

"Widowed?" Kristine could barely whisper. "Does she have other children?"

"She was married to a banker who died in a car accident. No, she doesn't have any other children besides you."

Tears welled in Kristine's eyes.

"When can I meet her?"

"You said you were traveling to Maryland soon, right?
I would advise you to visit her a day after you get into town.

Settle into your hotel and gather your thoughts before meeting her," Paulo said. "Are you ready to write down her address and phone number?"

"Yes," Kristine said as she reached for her notepad and pen.

Kristine's hand shook as she wrote down the contact information of her birth mom. Tears ran down her cheeks, but at the same time her heart leapt for joy as she realized that her greatest dream was coming true.

Kristine returned her phone to its cradle and bowed her head in prayer. She had to thank God because she knew He was the One who orchestrated this entire process. Her gratitude was beyond words, so for a while she simply wept.

~ * ~

Eric opened the door to his brick front three-story townhouse and locked it behind him.

It was ten o'clock at night, and he was starving.

Normally, Eric didn't eat dinner unless he was taking a girl out but tonight was an exception. He opened the refrigerator and took a look at the options: a carton of milk, a bottle of orange juice, bottled water, pasta, some fresh fruits and vegetables. He decided to take out the pasta and dice a few carrots to go with it.

Five minutes later, Eric was seated at his kitchen table, eating his meal. *It's not the Food Network, but it will do.*

As Eric finished, the telephone rang.

Eric took a gulp of water then answered the phone. "Good evening."

"Good evening, son."

Eric felt his heart drop to his stomach. "Dad." Eric managed his mixed emotions. "How are you?"

"Come home for Christmas and see for yourself," he said.

Eric began to think the worst. "Is everything okay?"

"Just come home for Christmas, son. We miss you."

"We?"

"Your mom and I are getting re-married a few days after Christmas."

It was the surprise of Eric's life. He didn't know whether to be overjoyed or overwhelmed. "That's great, Dad," he managed to say. "I'll see what I can do about visiting for the holidays."

"Good," Eric's dad said before hanging up the phone.

The dial tone sounded in Eric's ear, but he felt paralyzed. He didn't know if this was good or bad news. Slowly, Eric hung up the phone and tried to process through his thoughts.

Could it be that after all these years of separation there was hope for his parents?

~ * ~

Elle sat on the subway rail which would return her to the station where she'd parked her car. She'd taken the subway to her final scheduled interview because she was told that parking was hard to find. Elle had been an hour early to her interview as a grant writer for the National Endowment for the Arts.

The receptionist had let her sit in the lobby and read brochures while waiting.

Elle smiled. Mercedes Rivera, the hiring manager, had been impressed by Elle's early-bird approach to the interview— a fact which Elle hoped had earned her brownie points. The interview went well, and Mercedes said that she would call Elle before December twentieth to let her know if she got the job. Elle took out her cell phone and looked at the calendar. *Only three-and-a-half days until I know if I've landed my dream job!*

After spending ten minutes on the metro rail, Elle arrived at her destination. She stepped out into the chilly winter weather and walked briskly to her car.

Was it going to snow? It was awfully cold.

Elle sat in her BMW for a few minutes, waiting for it to warm-up so that she could turn the heat on. *Dear Jesus,* she prayed, *thank you for an eventful day. If it is Your will, please help me to land my dream job before the New Year.*

# Chapter 8

"Great, I've got a sprained ankle, *and* there's a snowstorm in Maryland?"

Derek laughed.

"What's so funny?"

"By the time we get to Maryland, the winter weather advisory will no longer be in effect. "And I'm used to driving in snow, so relax. We'll be fine."

"Do I have everything?" Kristine asked. "Where's my checklist?"

"On your kitchen table."

Kristine walked awkwardly to the kitchen. Her crutches had been replaced by a stability boot.

As she returned to her living room, she read the list aloud. "Gift bag with the picture frame for birth mom?"

"Check," Derek said.

"Suitcase full of clothes and essentials?"

"Check." Derek looked at the oversized pink suitcase. It held everything she needed and more.

"My purse?"

"Check."

"My photo albums?"

"Check."

"All right," Kristine said as she placed a checkmark next to the final item on the list. "Do you have everything?"

"I've got my wallet, my car keys, and you."

Kristine laughed. "Aw, how sweet."

"What are we waiting for?" Derek said. "Let's go."

He carried her to the car and gently helped her into the passenger's seat. He then loaded all the items into the back seat of his Jeep.

"Ready?" he asked after locking her townhouse and climbing into the driver's seat.

"Let's pray that this works out, Derek."

The couple bowed their heads in prayer then took off toward Maryland.

~ * ~

Eric walked into the office with a look of pure surprise on his face—a look he hadn't been able to erase since talking with his dad last night.

"Morning, Eric," Rebecca chirped then paused as he walked right past her and into his office.

Rebecca followed him. "Are you okay?"

"Yes," Eric said. "I think I am."

"Are you sure?"

"Do you really want to know?"

Rebecca paused, not knowing if this was a trick question. "I don't know."

"Have a seat."

Rebecca sat across from Eric's desk.

"My parents are back together."

Rebecca's eyes grew wide. When she first started working for Eric, he'd told her the reason he became a defense attorney in family law cases—it had something to do with hoping to settle bitter divorce disputes without destroying families. Rebecca noticed how he became sad every Christmas season as he wrestled with divorce cases. She intuitively knew that it had to be because of his parents' divorce or something that had happened in his past.

*Looks like Eric got his Christmas wish. If only I could get my Christmas wish. If only he'd take me out on a date.*

"Can you believe it?" he asked.

She smiled. "Yes, Eric, I can."

"How?"

"When you told me the story about your parents, it sounded like even though your dad was an alcoholic and brash at times, he still loved you and your mom."

"I just can't believe it."

"You should."

"Why?"

"Miracles happen."

"But you don't understand. My mom moved to Tahiti, okay? *Tahiti!*"

Rebecca just smiled. "God works in mysterious ways," she finally said. "You'd be surprised. When people are meant to be together, I believe it just works out."

"You're right," Eric said. "This is a miracle."

"I'm happy for you." She stood and return to her desk.

"Rebecca?" Eric called.

"Yes?"

"Pencil me out of town for the next two weeks. I'm leaving on Sunday to spend Christmas with my parents. And, Rebecca? Would you like to celebrate with me?"

Rebecca began to blush. "What do you mean?"

"I'm so happy that my parents are back together again that I forgot I'll need a wedding date."

"A wedding date?"

"Yes, ma'am."

"I'd love to be your wedding date."

"Great then pencil yourself out of town too. Book yourself a hotel room. I'll send you information for one near my parents. And don't worry about a rental car. I'll provide transportation for your entire stay."

Eric paused. "You don't already have plans, do you?"

Rebecca shook her head. "No."

"Great, we can celebrate together."

Rebecca smiled, silently exhilarated that she would be his date for the wedding but still nervous about how it would affect their work relationship. "I will be your wedding date, Eric. Thank you for the invitation."

He grinned. "Thanks, Rebecca. You're the best."

"So are you, Eric."

She then returned to her desk and sighed, then smiled and spun around in her chair for a good moment as she relished in the fact that her quiet hope to date Eric had finally come true.

~ * ~

"What do you mean I didn't get the job?" Elle asked, mortified.

"It means," Mercedes Rivera gently explained, "we chose someone whose skill set was a better match for our organization."

"But I was early to the interview, and you said that you liked my work."

"I'm sorry, Ms. Brighton, but someone has already been hired for the job. Happy Holidays."

Elle began to sob, only to realize that she was sobbing to a dial tone. She let the phone drop to the floor and she curled up in a fetal position on her hotel bed.

"What am I going to do?" she asked aloud. "I've been through all of my interviews. What now?"

A thought occurred to Elle. *Mandy Dawson gave me a business card that day at the gym!*

"The business card!" she said. "Where did I leave that business card?"

Elle began to search her entire hotel room for the card. An hour later, she still had not found it.

"Oh no," she said. "Did I put it in the trash?"

She dug through the waste baskets until at the bottom of one she found it, torn in two.

"What was I thinking?" She placed the torn pieces together. "Why would I waste a job opportunity?"

Elle retrieved the phone from the floor, sat in a chair, and dialed the number.

"Happy Holidays!" a friendly yet professional voice greeted. "Mandy Dawson speaking."

Elle paused.

"Hello?" Mandy said.

"Hi, Mandy, it's Elle Brighton, from the gym."

"Oh, Elle! Good afternoon! How can I help you?"

*You could give me a job. Please!* "I'd like to interview for that job opening."

"Great!" Mandy said. "We're closed for the holidays all of next week. But why don't you come in today? It's still early."

Elle's face lit up. "Really?"

"Sure. Let me check my agenda for the next opening."

Elle waited patiently for Mandy to check her schedule.

"I've an opening for three o'clock today. Think you can make it?"

"Yes!" Elle all but shouted. "I mean, yes, Mandy, I will be there."

After getting directions to the office building, Elle hung up the telephone with high expectations. Quickly, she prepared to go.

*Peace and Love*

# Chapter 9

E lle took a tour of the offices with Mandy Dawson as her tour guide.

"And this is our fashion apparel work room," Mandy said as she opened the door to reveal twenty students working at sewing machines, tables, and mannequins.

"Wow," Elle said, her eyes wide. "This is awesome."

"Yes, it is," Mandy agreed. "Our students are very dedicated designers—most with aspirations to become the next Versace or DKNY."

"Wow."

"So when can you start?" Mandy asked as she shut the door and continued walking with Elle, this time toward Mandy's office.

"Start? When?" Elle stopped in her tracks.

Mandy smiled. "We'd like to hire you."

"Are you kidding?"

"No."

"You're for real?" Elle squealed.

"Yes, we are for real."

Elle gave Mandy a big hug then took a step back. "Yes, I'd love to work for the Art Institute!"

"Great," Mandy said as they continued walking. "When can you start?"

"Well, I'm in town until New Year's, but I can definitely move here by January third. I can start immediately."

"Good," Mandy said as they stepped into her office. "We won't need you until the second week of January. We can assist you with relocation expenses."

Elle wanted to cry for joy, but she tried her best to contain her emotions.

*Thank you, Jesus!* She silently praised God for answering her prayers for a job.

"Have a seat," Mandy said. "You have papers to sign and a W-2 form to fill out."

Elle obeyed orders and began to sign the official papers.

Twenty minutes later, Elle gave the completed forms to Mandy and smiled. "Thank you so much, Ms. Dawson, for hiring me. I will not disappoint."

"Please, call me Mandy. We look forward to working with you." Mandy stood and walked with Elle to the door. "We'll call you after New Year's Day to talk relocation expenses and any other details we can assist you with during your move. Where are you moving from again?"

"Detroit."

Mandy nodded. "Good, our moving van can meet you on location in Michigan. But like I said, we'll call you to iron everything out."

Elle smiled and gave her new boss one more hug before leaving. "Thank you. I appreciate this so much."

"You're welcome, Elle. You'll do fine. I'm sure of it."

"Happy Holidays!" Elle told Mandy before walking toward the elevator.

"Thank you," Mandy returned. "Have a merry Christmas!"

"I will!" Elle called over her shoulder. *Now. Thank You, Jesus, for dreams come true.*

~ * ~

Kristine quietly approached the door to the home where Paulo said her mother lived. It was two days before Christmas, and Kristine hoped her mother was still home and not out shopping for the holidays.

*If she's anything like me,* Kristine thought, *she's shopping right now.*

Despite her negative thoughts, Kristine got up the nerve to ring the doorbell. She wished Derek were with her.

Kristine was beginning to doubt her decision to keep Derek and the news of her engagement at bay until she had a chance to meet and speak with her mother. Derek had supported her decision, saying it might be too much at once for someone who hadn't seen her since giving birth.

After waiting two minutes, Kristine rang the doorbell again. Tears began to well up in her eyes.

*I guess she's not home,* Kristine thought.

Just as she turned to leave, the door opened and a voice called after her. "Excuse me!"

A startled Kristine spun around.

"What are you doing on my —" the lady started then stared.

Kristine looked at a carbon copy of herself—only about two decades older. "Mom?"

"Oh my," Colleen said as she approached the younger version of herself.

"I'm your daughter."

"You look just like me," Colleen observed as she touched the hair of her baby girl all grown up.

Kristine began to cry. "All my life I've dreamed of meeting you—and asking why. Why didn't you keep me?"

Tears welled up in Colleen's eyes as she felt her daughter's pain. It echoed her own pain which she kept buried deep inside, until this moment. Colleen gave her daughter a hug. "I was too young and didn't have the money to give you the life you deserved. But I hope I can now."

"I didn't want your money," Kristine sobbed. "I just wanted you."

Colleen stepped back and wiped her tears away. "Well," she said with a smile, "now that you've found me, I believe we have a lot of catching up to do."

Kristine's tears of sadness transformed into tears of joy as the reality of reuniting with her birth mom began to settle in. Kristine noticed that Colleen was dressed to brave the weather in a wool coat, hat, and boots with a purse over her shoulder. "Were you about to leave?"

"I was about to do some last minute Christmas shopping," Colleen admitted before smiling and looped her arm through Kristine's. "But shopping can wait. Besides, I believe that God's already sent my Christmas gift to me. In fact, He's delivered you right to my doorstep."

Kristine laughed. "I bought you a gift too," Kristine said as she held up a pretty bag decorated with glittering snowflakes.

"It's beautiful," Colleen remarked. She caught Kristine's hand. "Is that a diamond ring?"

Kristine blushed. She'd meant to remove the ring until after she'd told her mother the news. "I meant to tell you. But I just found you, and I didn't want to overwhelm you with news."

Colleen shivered from the cold. "Come on inside. I believe we've got a lot of catching up to do."

~ ✱ ~

Eric walked up the walkway to his father's house in Seattle.

He loved the scent of pine trees that lined the walkway.

Now standing at the front door, Eric knocked.

"Eric!" a happy feminine voice cried as the door opened.

Eric took a step back. "Mom?"

"Welcome home, baby," she said, reaching out to give her son a hug.

Eric stepped to the side, not fully ready to reconcile with the woman who'd abandoned him. "I thought you moved to Tahiti."

"I did. But your father didn't tell you?"

"Maria, I haven't talked to the boy in an entire decade." His dad appeared at his ex-wife's side.

"Hi, Dad," Eric said. "I'm sorry that I—"

"Aw, hush your fuss," the elderly man said as he greeted his son with a hug. "You're our son. We'll always love you."

The warmth of the holiday season and the good news of his parents' reconciliation filled Eric's heart with love and peace.

"Now come inside, Eric," his mom said. "You'll catch a cold standing out here."

Eric followed his mother's orders.

"Would you like some eggnog?" Dad inquired.

"No, sir. I don't drink."

"Nor do I!"

"It's non-alcoholic," Maria explained.

"Now we aren't going to quarrel anymore," he said, referring to his ex-wife. "We're getting married again on New Year's Eve."

"I think that's wonderful, Dad."

"Who are you bringing to the wedding?"

"Her name is Rebecca," Eric said. "She's my paralegal."

"Para-what?"

"Legal secretary," Eric explained.

"Oh!" his mother laughed. "I thought that was a fancy term for saying she's your soul mate."

Eric laughed. "No, Mom, it's strictly business."

"Are you sure?"

Eric paused. "I don't know," he confessed. "I'm not doing too well with the dating thing."

"Take it from us." Dad took a swing of eggnog. "If your mother and I can work it out, you can find true love and work it out too."

"Now what is that supposed to mean?" Maria asked, taking offense.

"It just means that we were meant to be together all along, but you had to go chasing your dreams elsewhere."

"Now, Elmer David, you know that's simply not true!"

"Well, what is woman? You left me for Tahiti!"

"Maybe if you weren't always drinking, we'd never had divorced!"

"Why did we divorce anyway?"

"I just told you."

"Woman, I—"

"Elmer, you—" Maria started, but her voice was silenced as Elmer kissed her lips. A deep blush rose on Maria's face as she pushed him away. "You romantic rascal, you."

"You brilliant, beautiful woman, you," Elmer bantered as he moved in for another kiss.

Eric watched his parents interact with renewed hope in his heart. It looked like they'd sorted out their problems and were ready to commit for what Eric hoped would be forever.

Suddenly they stopped their interaction and engulfed their son in a bear hug. "Merry Christmas, son," they said. "We love you."

"I love you too," Eric said, grateful that after so many years he would have a truly merry Christmas. "Here's to peace and love." He raised a glass of eggnog to toast.

"Peace and love," his parents echoed as they touched their glasses to Eric's.

It truly was a Christmas to remember.

# *Peace and Love*

# Epilogue

*D*ear God,

*'Tis the season to be joyful, thankful for our blessings and filled with love and peace. Thank You, Jesus, for blessing me with family—adoptive, new, and old.*

*My birth mother and I talked and shared photo albums until sunrise. I've never been that long without sleep. Derek called me because he was worried that I wasn't answering the phone at the hotel. I told him that I spent the night at my mom's house. He sounded happy that I was happy, and my mom wanted to see the man who "makes me glow" so she invited my Derek over for Christmas dinner.*

*My mom said that I'll get to meet the rest of my family today—they're all coming over for Christmas dinner.*

*I'm so happy! Reconciling with my birth mom is the very best gift You've ever given me, dear Lord—apart from my adoptive parents and, of course, Derek!* ☺

*I love You, Lord. Thank You again for all the blessings You've showered on me and my loved ones.*

*And for the gift of Your Son without Whom we have no life.*

*Merry Christmas, Jesus.*

*Peace and Love,*

*Kristine.*

Dear God,

I haven't written out a prayer to You in a while, and for that I do apologize.

But I've found even more reason to write prayer notes to You because it's in times like these I realize how much You've been and continue to be there for me and my family.

Thank You for helping my parents find it in their hearts to forgive each other and to realize how much they still love each other. And thank You for enabling me to be alive to witness their wedding—a renewal of their vows.

Thank you for Rebecca, who so graciously agreed to be my wedding date. I like her a lot. She's nothing like the other women I usually fall for. Rebecca's more the quiet type who excels in the workplace but is shy around men. I hope to change that. She's what I need—not a supermodel, drama queen, diva, NFL cheerleader, or any of the type I usually date.

Maybe the reason I've failed miserably at finding the right girl is because I've been ignoring the right girl for me. And she's been under my nose for the past two years. Now that I realize this, I'm not going to let her go—though she may have to get a new job since couples aren't allowed to work together in our firm.

Thank You for working out the Bridget Andersen case! Rebecca called me from the office before she left for Seattle, saying that Bridget no longer wants a divorce. Apparently Mr. Andersen checked himself into rehab and therapy. He realized during their separation that he loved her more than his bad habits. They've reached an agreement— he'll drop all of his bad habits through therapy, and she'll attend marriage counseling with him. It sounds like they're going to work it out.

I may even receive an invitation to the renewing of their vows.

My phone's ringing. It's Rebecca. She's at the airport, wondering where I am.

*I've got to pick her up. After all, I promised to provide her transportation during her stay.*

*Thank You again, Jesus. I love You.*
*Peace and Love,*
*Eric.*

~ * ~

*Dear God,*

*Wow, just wow!*

*You've blessed me with a new job for the New Year! Thank You so much!*

*Aunt Charlotte and my cousins rejoiced at my news. They're just as happy as I am. Maybe they were a bit worried. I know I was! But I am happy that I realize now more than ever why You have told us in the Bible not to worry. You take care of the sparrow; certainly You'll take care of us.*

*Thank You! Thank You! Thank You!*

*I love You, Lord, with all my heart.*

*Merry Christmas.*
*Peace and Love (and a thankful heart),*
*Elle.*

— *The End* —

CPSIA information can be obtained at www.ICGtesting.com
Printed in the USA
BVOW05s1652291014

372866BV00001B/38/P